NAUGHTY & NICE GIFT ANTHOLOGY

THREE HOLIDAY ROMANCE NOVELLAS

LEE SAVINO

SNOWED IN WITH MY GROUCHY BOSS

What's worse than getting snowed in on Christmas with the Dread Lord, a.k.a. my awful and (annoyingly) sexy boss? When he walks in on me enjoying "me" time in the hot tub... whilst I'm nekkid.

CHAPTER 1

The mountain mansion is straight out of a luxury magazine or a pretty Christmas snow globe. Candles glow in the windows. The slate roof looks like it was dusted with sugar. I'd feel like I'm in a winter wonderland if an icy wind wasn't chasing me up the drive.

Snow is piled up on either side of the driveway in giant white drifts taller than me, and the wind is driving more fluffy white flakes into my face. Only a madman would be out in this weather. Or a poor, put-upon employee of Mr. Lord, who is basically The Grinch and Ebenezer Scrooge rolled into one.

Dear Santa, please keep me from dying on this hill.

The drive is made of old-fashioned cobblestones, which is quaint and all, but a nightmare to walk on in high-heeled boots. I would've dressed differently if I'd known my boss was going to drag me to the North Pole on the night before Christmas Eve.

I'm going to kill him. All this snow would hide his body until at least May.

The heel of my boot hits a patch of black ice, and I go

flying. My body goes one way, my suitcase another, while I squawk like a chicken, bracing for impact.

Out of nowhere, two strong arms catch and lift me upright. For a second, my boss holds me against his powerful body. His body heat seeps into me, and I think, *Maybe he's not the Iceman; maybe he is human,* but then he opens his mouth.

"Careful," he clips in his posh British accent. "If you fall and break a leg, you'll be useless at work. And then where will we be?"

"Home for Christmas," I mutter. "Where we should be."

He sets me on my feet, and I turn in time to see the surprised flick of his dark eyebrows. He's used to my snark. We snipe at each other like an old married couple, but usually I try to act professional or, at least, tone down my crazy.

But tonight? Six p.m. on the Friday before a holiday weekend? All my fucks are gone.

I don't feel bad because Piers Lord, a.k.a. the Dread Lord, gives as good as he gets.

"Home? In your tiny apartment with the broken radiator you're always complaining about?" His British accent always makes him sound like he's sneering. Sometimes I can't tell if he's mocking me, but right now it's clear: he's mocking me. "Eating fruit cake and watching cat show competitions on your sad little telly?"

"That sounds perfect." I glare up at him. He's still holding me close, so I push at his chest to get some distance between us. He's packing some serious muscle underneath his wool pea coat, and I fit perfectly in his arms, but I ignore the flush of heat between my legs.

If life were fair, my boss would have green, gangrenous skin and look like a troll to match his repulsive personality. But the Dread Lord is the result of several generations of wealthy people marrying hot people. His dad was a British tycoon, and his mom was a Miss World pageant winner turned Bollywood star. He was destined to win the hotness lottery.

It's not easy working for a man who has the money of Midas and the face and body of a god. I'm careful not to look at him for too long, lest I get mesmerized by his pouty mouth and pointy cheekbones. After almost five years, you think I'd be used to it, but nope.

He cocks his head, and his silky black hair falls across his obnoxiously perfect brow. "But then you wouldn't be here. With me."

"That sounds even better."

"You'd miss this lovely weather." He sniffs at the dark gray sky, and I can't tell if he's joking. Sometimes I think he prefers it when the world is gloomy, covered in a shroud.

He's still holding me close, so close I'm warmed by the heat of his body. If I close my eyes, I could pretend that my fantasies are coming true.

Because, let's face it, I fantasize about my hot boss all the time. It's a problem.

The hardest part of this job isn't dealing with the Dread Lord's razor-sharp tongue or demanding standards. I don't mind those; I love a challenge. Marty used to say I was the only one who could handle Piers. I've lasted longer than all his other assistants combined.

No, the hardest part is how much I'm attracted to him. Not just his gorgeous face and powerful body, but his brilliant mind, his cutting wit. It's not fair that I'm into someone so mean, but... I like him best when he's mean.

Dear Santa,

Help.

Right now, my body can't help but respond to his. But I am not going to give in to my ridiculous attraction and enjoy the moment. I refuse! It's just that it's been a long time since

I've been with a man, or anyone, and my body is hungry for human touch.

"I don't understand why we needed to come all the way to the North Pole for a work day," I mutter.

"Vermont is not the North Pole. We're nearly twenty-five hundred kilometers from the Arctic Circle."

"What's that in miles?" I ask because any reference to *nonsensical American metrics* drives him crazy.

I reach for my suitcase, but the Dread Lord lifts it out of my reach. I slip and nearly fall again. He catches me with his free hand, and without any apparent effort, he guides me and my suitcase all the way to the grand oak doors.

"Don't worry, Wellesley, you'll be home for Christmas. We'll be done with the deal with All Cap by midnight. The jet will return you to your hovel, where you can dine on cold Chinese takeout and watch horrible holiday movies to your heart's content."

I press my lips together to suppress a grin. Maybe I have some wires crossed, but getting roasted by the Dread Lord only leaves me warm and toasty.

Besides, he's right about the cold Chinese takeout. His zingers aren't just eloquent, they're accurate, which is why they truly sting. If I were home, I would be eating leftovers in front of the TV. I'll never admit it, but I'd also probably still be on my laptop. I have to stay on top of my inbox in my off hours, or I'd be buried under an avalanche of emails every Monday morning.

"Thank you, milord." I feign a Cockney accent. If he wasn't propping me up, I'd drop into a curtsey just to annoy him.

"Cheeky peasant."

My insides warm like I've drunk mulled wine. I love our inside jokes. Piers pretends he hates them, of course, but that's part of the fun.

He mutters something under his breath about 'a poor excuse for picking a man's pocket every twenty-fifth of December.' I think he's actually quoting directly from Dickens, so props to him.

Once we're inside the house, the warmth embraces me, and I can breathe again. Now that I'm not turning into an icicle, I can appreciate how beautiful the mansion is. The entryway opens to a sitting room with couches and lounge chairs in front of a wall of windows. The caretaker must have just left, because a fire is crackling in the huge stone fireplace.

"Wow," I say. "This is amazing."

The Dread Lord frowns, looking around like he's missed something.

I gesture to the cozy-looking couches and the snowy landscape showcased by three stories of glass. "The house. The view. This place is beautiful."

He stalks forward, facing the big picture windows. In his black pea coat and big leather gloves, his copper skin glowing in the firelight, he looks like a true Dread Lord surveying his kingdom. "I suppose it will do."

Of course, he's not impressed. He's used to this sort of luxury. He was born into wealth, emancipated from his parents at age seventeen to access his trust and 10xed his net worth since then. Working for him means travelling via private jet to some of the best and most beautiful cities and buildings in the world, but I hope I never get used to it.

The caretaker also took care to remove any holiday decor, as per my hastily emailed instructions three hours ago. There's not a sign of a Christmas tree, tinsel, or mistletoe. No signs of Hanukkah, like dreidels or a menorah, either.

I'm patting myself on the back for making sure nothing would incur the Dread Lord's wrath, when I notice his back has stiffened. He's staring at something outside the windows, and I hurry over to see what it is.

A huge fir tree stands alone on the slope beyond the over-sized wooden deck. It has to be over forty feet tall, and it's covered in colorful lights that shine against the gray sky.

Oh well. The caretaker removed most of the holiday decor.

My boss's face has turned to stone. His lips press together as he glares at the tree like his eyes are about to shoot lasers and incinerate the last sign of festive cheer.

"Do you want me to run out there and rip down the lights?" I ask, and hold my breath. Because if he says yes, I'll have to do it, and I have no idea how to levitate forty feet in the air.

He presses his lips together and shakes his head. Internally, I breathe a sigh of relief.

I love Christmas. My mom and I didn't have much growing up, but she always made the holidays special.

From what I can gather, the Dread Lord has no fond memories of this time of year. His parents had a frosty divorce, and once it was done, they immediately started new families and ignored the son they had made together. I imagine the Dread Lord as a little boy, abandoned at boarding school all winter. Forgotten by his family.

But maybe it's time to make new memories. That's where I come in.

"I guess this is as good a time as any for this." I unzip the front pocket of my suitcase, pull out a Santa hat, and put it on. "Tada! A bit of holiday cheer."

The Dread Lord looks at me like I just killed a kitten in front of him.

"I got one for you, too." I pull out a second hat and hold it out to him. I'm risking my life here, but it's worth it to see him trying to hide his shock.

"No."

"Oh, come on." I shake the hat at him. "You know you want to. 'Tis the season."

For a second, he hesitates. He actually hesitates! Like he's considering it.

I have many Dread Lord fantasies that've gotten me through the past five years. The most delusional is that, deep in the depths of his black heart, Piers Lord enjoys my relentless cheer. I'm the sunshine to his grumpy, the golden retriever to his black cat. He complains, but he knows he needs me to bring a little light into his life.

And I love that. I love being his little light bringer. I make it my personal mission to add a dash of joy to our sixteen-hour work days, and it's working. The Dread Lord eats, breathes, and sweats money, but he's been lightening up a little since Marty died.

So this moment, where he's considering dressing up for a holiday he loathes just for me? I'll treasure it.

All too soon, the moment ends.

"Absolutely not."

"Can I at least wear mine?"

"Only if you want it to end up feeding the fire."

I gasp. He wouldn't really throw my hat on the fire, would he? I decide not to risk it and tuck both hats away. "Bah humbug," I whisper.

"What was that?"

"Nothing. I was singing a Christmas carol." I hum a few bars of "Kiss Me Like It's Christmas."

"Well, stop it."

So, not only is he not going to enjoy the Christmas spirit, he's going to suck the joy out of me, too? Just another day in the life of the Dread Lord's lowly assistant.

If I had time to have friends, they'd ask me why I don't quit. My massage therapist asked me once after she dug the boulders out of my shoulders. I told her that I barely graduated high school, but I make bank being the administrative assistant to the devil.

At least it's warm in hell.

"You know, some people get Christmas off," I say.

"You do get Christmas off." Piers helps me with my coat, his smirk making a mockery of his etiquette.

"The whole weekend." I resist the urge to stop my boots on the maple parquet floor. "Christmas Eve and Christmas."

He turns from hanging our coats in the closet and stalks toward me, his gaze running up and down my body. His mother's eyes are famous, a light brown that was almost golden, and the Dread Lord inherited them, down to the long, black lashes.

I keep my chin high, resisting the urge to shrink back. He can't find fault with my outfit. This job gives me an unlimited wardrobe budget, and I've always used it, mostly at brands in the Lord Ltd. portfolio. But for the past few months, I've worked hard to glow up even more. My flawless skin, hair, makeup, and clothes are my armor.

Everyone's noticed… except the Dread Lord. I tell myself it doesn't matter; I didn't do it for him.

But I'm lying. My only consolation is that, if he's that oblivious to me, he hasn't noticed my pathetic crush.

The Dread Lord is still looking me up and down. I know he's searching for weakness, but a part of me is preening. He has this way of focusing on someone so they feel like they're the only person in the world. It's a superpower, and I'm by no means immune. Tingles spread over my body. I keep my face composed, but inside, I'm ready to combust.

Dear Santa, please keep my nipples from showing through this sweater dress.

Finally, he finds something to criticize. "Red boots?"

"For Christmas." I pose with exaggerated cheer. I love my

bright red boots. They're the height of fashion but also scream, "Don't fuck with me, or I'll drive this stiletto through your eyeball." Which is the sort of sartorial statement I like to make when I'm at work.

He presses his lips together but doesn't respond. He's looking intently at me, and again, I fight the urge to squirm. I've spent four years, eleven months, and twenty-six days tuning into his moods so I can read all his expressions, but I've never seen this one before.

I can't stand the intensity of his scrutiny, so I turn to the wall of windows. Outside, the snow is falling faster. *Storm of the century,* all the headlines said.

I bite my lip. "They're calling for more inches."

"I've never known anyone to complain of more inches," he mutters.

Sweet Santa, did he just make a dirty joke? I stifle my laugh just in time. There's a prickle between my legs, but more than that, I feel giddy. He's relaxing a bit, letting down his walls. Letting his personality peek out. Maybe coming to this house was a good idea. "More isn't always better."

"Oh, Wellesley, you must know by now that more isn't just better, it's the best. Never settle for less, darling."

Darling?

He moves so he's standing right behind me. If I backed up a little to the left, I'd be in his arms again.

I take a deep inhale of his signature cologne. It's woodsy and fresh with notes of birch and vetiver, and also hints of something sweet, like pineapple. It's the sexiest thing I've ever smelled. I want to roll around in it and rub myself against him.

We're cozied up together in a beautiful mansion with only a few inches of space between us. This is basically the start to my Dread Lord Fantasy No. Seventy-Five, the one where he has a black turtleneck and calls me something endearing, like 'sweetheart.' *Darling.* He still has his cutting wit, but he's kind to me. Until he rips my clothes off and fucks me on the floor.

Or was it the bed? The floor might be Fantasy No. Seventy Six.

That's right, I've fantasized about my boss so much that I've catalogued them. It's bad.

But it doesn't matter, because my fantasies will never, ever happen.

"You know, this is the perfect sort of place to take a vacation," I venture. "Some time off. No meetings, no email."

"Oh? And just who would be on this vacation with me?" He murmurs over my shoulder. The fine hairs on my neck stand at attention.

I fight to keep my voice steady. "A few friends."

"Friends?" His gentle touch on my elbow turns me to face him. I'm still in my heeled boots, yet he towers over me. His face is blank, but his tone is self-deprecating. "What friends?"

Oh, right, he doesn't have friends. Not since Marty passed.

"Maybe a… lady friend?" My heart is thumping so loud, he can probably hear it. I can't believe I'm being so bold. I can't believe he's standing so close to me. If I lean in, I could lay my head on his chest. *Fantasy No. Sixty Two.* I'm aching for it.

"Lady friend?" His voice is low, almost a purr. "Who would you recommend?"

I can't focus. He's looking at me too intently. I lick my lips, and his gaze drops to my mouth.

Then I remember the tall blonde who strides into his office every Tuesday at two, and the warm fuzzy feelings disappear like I've been splashed with ice water. I could mention 'Scary Sandra,' but I don't want to. The thought of him coming here with her makes me want to puke.

I've reluctantly accepted the fact that she's the woman he's chosen because who wouldn't choose her? She's striking, elegant, and put together.

Pretty much the opposite of me.

I take a few steps back, keeping my voice breezy. "Oh, I'm sure you can find someone to tolerate you. Lots of ladies would like to cozy up to your bank account." I can't believe I'm being so cheeky, but the crinkles around his eyes tell me he's enjoying it.

"I don't want them," he says, and I feel even warmer. If this were Fantasy No. Twenty-Two, he'd say *I want you,* right before ripping my clothes off and fucking me hard in front of the fireplace.

Never gonna happen.

I clear my throat. "Maybe you'll meet one at the Thruster's New Year's party."

His expression changes so quickly, I get whiplash. A storm cloud passes over his face.

"Enough dawdling." His icy tone makes me shiver. "Let's get to work." He spins on his heel and strides away.

I stand frozen, cold to the bone. *What just happened?* For a moment, we were flirting just like in my fantasies, but it was real and wonderful. And then he just… changed.

What did I say?

"Hurry up, Wellesley," he barks. He's halfway down the hall. "Shanghai opens in ninety minutes."

So much for spreading holiday cheer. I set aside my sinking spirits, grab the laptop bag, and scurry after him.

Only five and a half more hours, then I can go home.

CHAPTER 2

*L*ight blazes in my face, too white and too bright. I surface from sleep in stages. I'm in a California king bed, lying with my head turned toward the window. The blinds are up, and the sun is blazing over the mountains, the rays bouncing off the snow, blinding.

I sit up, wiping drool from my mouth. I'm still wearing my sweater dress and Christmas kitten socks, but my boots are off. I remember sneaking my bra off around ten last night and hoping the Dread Lord wouldn't notice how loose my boobs were under my dress. But I don't remember leaving the workroom or climbing into a bed. Someone must have carried me upstairs and tucked me in.

Piers must have. He's the only one here. That was… kind. Not very "Dread Lord" of him at all.

Then I realize what I'm looking at. The lone Christmas tree outside is covered in mounds of fluffy white, but I don't remember that much snow on it the night before.

"Oh no. No, no no no nono," I chant under my breath as I run downstairs. My socks make me skid on the polished wood floors, so I crash into the front door.

I pull it open and stare in dismay at the snow piled outside the door. The driveway is covered with at least two feet of snow.

How did it snow this much? I thought *Storm of the Century* was a hyperbole.

My last memory from last night was tiptoing to the windows to peek behind the blinds. The sliver of glass showed thick snowflakes falling at a furious rate. I remember feeling despair, then hope because Piers told me he'd make sure I was home for Christmas.

Now I have the sinking feeling that he was wrong.

"Wellesley?"

Speak of the Dread Lord, and he shall appear. He's still in his suit, although he's taken off his suit jacket. His white button-down is no more rumpled than it was last night, and not one strand of his glossy black hair is out of place.

Whereas I'm sure I look like something a cat puked up. I don't need to glance at a mirror to know I look a mess. I get horrible bedhead, like I've been electrocuted, and day-old mascara always gives me raccoon eyes.

To his credit, the Dread Lord doesn't react with disgust at my appearance. He frowns at the open door. "What are you doing?"

I'm hyperventilating, too upset to speak. This isn't like me. I don't usually lose it like this. The high stakes of my job have taught me how to hide my feelings. Inside, I'm a bunch of ADHD-and-anxiety-ridden squirrel in a trench coat, but outside, I am zen.

But not today. Right now, I'm on the verge of a full-blown freakout. *I'm supposed to be home for Christmas.* Instead of answering my boss, I look out at the snowy drive and then back at him.

"There are easier ways to check the weather." He pulls out his phone and glances at it. "Seems we got six inches per hour. Broke a few records. I checked with the plows. They're stuck."

"Stuck," I repeat. "The snow plows."

"It's quite a bit of snow."

The heat vent by the door is blasting hot air on my head, but it doesn't stop the icy wind from blowing through me. I'm too cold to even shiver. My hand is about to freeze to the doorknob, but I can't move. My brain is glitching. "We're snowed in. You said I'd be able to go home today."

"Come now, Wellesley. I know you think I am all-powerful, but even I don't control the weather."

"You were wrong, and you're never wrong. I trusted you." My lower lip trembles. "You said I would be able to go home for Christmas. You promised." I sound like I'm five, but I can't help it. I feel like I'm five and finding out Santa isn't real.

It's ridiculous. I should never have believed him. But I did. I put my faith in him.

And he betrayed me.

"Close the door, Wellesley, it's freezing."

I slam the door so hard it bounces open again. A little snow falls on the beautiful wood floors. Normally, I'd feel bad about that, but I'm too upset.

The Dread Lord mutters something to himself as he prowls forward. I move out of his way, and he closes and locks the door.

"You're shivering," he chides.

I don't feel the cold. I'm filled with red-hot rage. The flames of hell are crackling behind my eyes.

The crazy has come.

I spent all yesterday holding it back because I didn't get to go home, and now… I can't hold back anymore. All my crazy is about to spew out of me. The mask is off.

I point at him. "You," I snarl. I sound demonic.

He raises a brow.

"You did this on purpose."

There it is—a flash of something cracking his world-renowned poker face. Regret, maybe? Guilt?

I don't care.

I'm done reading him. His moods, his whims, his needs... I've catalogued everything about him for four years, eleven months, and twenty-six days, and no more! It doesn't matter how hot he is. How much I live for his zingers and stern reprimands. I've studied his microexpressions and read way, way too much into them… for the last time!

"I give you everything. I only asked for one thing—one thing! But noooo. You're so miserable, you can't stand the holidays. And you're such a Grinch, you can't stand for anyone else to be happy. You want to drag me down with you. Well, not today, Satan. Not today and not any day hereafter!"

Now he's raised both of his brows. I sound deranged, but dammit, I don't care.

My fingers are cold and stiff, and it takes a few tries, but I pry open the clasp of the limited edition Rolex he bought for me on the first anniversary of our working together and hold it out to him.

"What is this?" His poker face is back.

"I'm done," I say, shaking the watch at him. "No more late nights. No more working lunches. No more missed weekends because you just had to fly to Shanghai on Friday. Take it."

"That was a gift."

"And I'm returning it."

He makes no move to take the watch, so I set it down on a side table. I could sell it for a few hundred thousand dollars, but pride dictates that I give it back.

Good riddance.

No, not good riddance. Bad riddance. The worst riddance.

A pox on him and his house!

I spin on my heel and march away.

"Where are you going?" the Dread Lord calls after me. Ideally, his voice would be tinged with worry, but no, his tone is still perfectly bland. He doesn't care about me. He never has.

And I'm done pretending it doesn't hurt.

"Anywhere away from you." Now I sound like a teenager. I march into the closest room, a dining room with a mahogany table that could seat twenty, and slam the door so hard I hear a picture frame fall in the hall.

Then I change my mind and reopen the door to walk back into the foyer. It ruins my grand exit, but I don't care. I ignore Piers and head to the closet to pull out my coat.

"I'm leaving." I move to the front door. The cold metal burns my palm, but I tug and tug until I remember he locked it.

I need to get it together. I'm so incensed, I'm not thinking clearly, and I need all my wits to stand against the Dread Lord.

His hand slams against the door before I can undo the lock and try again. "Wellesley, be sensible. You can't leave. I arranged for a helicopter to pick you up, but the pilot is still snowed in. The roads won't open for at least a day."

"Then I'll walk to the village." I'm making threats I can't follow through on, but this is a matter of pride.

"In your Christmas kitten socks?" He glances down at my feet. He doesn't smirk, but my skin prickles in embarrassment anyway.

"If I have to." It's not like my red boots will be any better. If anything, they'll kill me faster.

There has to be a pair of snowshoes around here somewhere. I'd be lucky if I was able to walk a foot in them, much less miles and miles.

"You'll risk loss of limb and life, and for what? To prove you can do it? To defy me?"

He's right. He's not worth getting hypothermia for. I hold onto the hot heat of my anger because I can't show how hurt I am.

It's not like I had big holiday plans. Just the usual: lounging around my apartment, cursing my finicky radiator, working on my email, then taking the subway to Rockefeller Center to buy an overpriced hot chocolate and people-watch—the way I used to do with my mom when she was alive.

It's not fancy, but it was our tradition. And now it's all I have.

I thought about changing it up this year, but I didn't realize I wouldn't have a choice.

And now here's the Dread Lord, looking smug, like he's glad I'm stuck here.

"You can't quit," he says.

My resolve hardens to titanium.

"I require several months' notice." He looks down his nose at me. "Perhaps longer. A few years."

"I got your notice, right here." I show him the middle finger of my right hand. I add my left hand, for good measure. *That's right! Double bird, baby!*

The Dread Lord's face is still blank, but his eyes burn like coals. He's not happy.

"You got it?" I ask sweetly, then stomp away.

I can't believe he did this to me. Actually, I can. He has no regard for anyone's feelings but his own.

There was a time after Marty's funeral that I thought he had a heart. He was kinder for a few months. Almost human. After a particularly grueling weekend where we found a workaround to the new U.S. tariffs, he even thanked and complimented me.

Well, not vocally. But his expression did soften, and he gave me a nod that I took to mean, *Well done, Welelsley.*

But it didn't last. This Tuesday, I didn't read his mind in time to reschedule his personal trainer, and he nearly took my head off.

It doesn't matter that he's hot. It doesn't matter that his insults are better crafted than most people's compliments. It doesn't matter that the perks of the job are awesome. I can give up the private chef and unlimited credit at the fashion houses in the Lord Ltd. portfolio. It was nice watching Thrusters games from the owner's box. My mother was always a Thrusters fan, so when Piers bought the team, it was like a dream come true.

I'm done.

I head in the direction of the kitchen. I need breakfast first, and there's something labelled "Nantucket pie" in the fridge. I don't know what that is, but the glazed cranberries on top looked delicious.

I don't go far because on the way, I find a speakeasy-style room with a full liquor bar. I'm not much of a drinker. I've had plenty of opportunities at fancy dinners, galas, and grand openings of this or that museum or opera house, but I'm always working, so I never imbibe.

But I'm a free woman now, so... seventy-five-year-old scotch? Don't mind if I do.

Before I can find a proper Glencairn glass, the Dread Lord finds me.

The hairs on my neck stand up, but I refuse to turn around and acknowledge him. He calls my name, and his voice is soft, caressing.

Is he trying to charm me? After I flipped him a double bird?

I don't trust it.

He steps close. The scent of his cologne, along with his body heat, surrounds me. He's so warm. I close my eyes against this assault on my senses and elbow him in the ribs.

Mistake. His abs are as hard as marble, so all I do is bang my funny bone. "Ow."

He turns me around, a frown creasing his handsome face. "Are you all right?"

"No." It annoys me that he's pretending to care. "Go away." I whirl and grab a crystal highball glass. Liquid courage, that's what they call it, right? That's what I need so I can stand up to him.

I grab the first bottle within reach. My hand shakes as I pour, but I fill the glass to the brim. "You are a Grinch, and it's time I treated you that way. You're hopeless."

I take a sip of my drink and start coughing. This is top-shelf alcohol? It burns!

I shove the glass away and grab a bottle of Baileys. Yes, whiskey and sweet cream. I can handle that.

"Wellesley," he murmurs. His hot breath hits the back of my neck. He's standing right behind me.

Santa, make me strong!

I'm tempted to do something drastic, something I've always wanted to do: Kiss my boss. Kiss the effing hell outta him. Then bite his beautiful upper lip.

That'll teach him! I'm going to do it if he doesn't back off.

But he's going to back off. That's what he does.

It'll be over soon, I tell myself. *You're going to show him all your weirdness, and that will drive him away.* I tell myself I won't be disappointed when that happens.

No, I will annoy him on purpose. He trapped me here, and I'm going to make him regret it.

"Did All Cap make you an offer? Is that what this is?" he

murmurs right into my ear. "Whatever they're offering, I'll double it. No, triple. Salary, benefits, stock options—"

"Time off? For all major holidays?" My tone is so dry, I risk dehydration.

He falls silent. Of course he does. He has nothing to say to that. The fucker.

He stole Christmas from me!

I pour some Baileys and drink a little before I risk turning around. Like always, his handsomeness stops my breath, but I let my anger burn my desire away. "No, I'm not going to work for your competitor. I'm not going to work at all. I've been saving my salary all these years. And I shorted that big tech stock everyone's been talking about."

His eyes narrow. I know that calculating look. He's planning on buying the tech company, which will run up the price and turn my windfall into peanuts.

"Don't even think about it." I gesture with my glass. "I've already moved that money to bonds. Treasuries." He won't be able to destabilize an entire country's economy. A small nation's, maybe.

"You can't possibly have enough to retire."

"I can if I budget. And I'm going to sell my clothes. I won't need a high-fashion work wardrobe where I'm going."

"Where are you going? A nudist colony?"

"Wouldn't you like to know." I roll my eyes. Consigning my designer boots and handbags will hopefully give me some extra cash to travel the world. I'm looking forward to wearing T-shirts and soft pants all day, every day.

"Whatever you've saved, it cannot possibly last." His golden eyes burn into me, and I'm at risk of losing lung function, so I stare at a point above his left ear.

"I don't know," I murmur into my glass. I've only had a few sips, but I feel warm and fuzzy. "The market's done very well. Don't worry, I'm keeping my Lord Ltd. stock." Always bet on the Dread Lord. Marty taught me that. Everything he touches turns to gold. "The company's growth is one of the reasons I'm able to retire so young," I add, to twist the knife further.

"A million?" he muses. "Maybe one point three. You can't have saved more than that."

I hold my breath, because he's right.

"You can't live on that."

"I can." It's called geo-arbitrage, but I'm not going to tell him that because I don't want him to know where I'm going. I'm going to travel, starting with Bangkok or Addis Ababa.

"Not in New York."

I freeze. I can't let him discover my plan. "I can if I eat lentils."

"Lentils."

"Yeah. I like lentils."

"No, you don't." His voice turns condescending. "You used to bring in that gruel every day for lunch. Homemade lentil stew. At the start of the week, you'd be able to choke it down, but by Thursday, you wouldn't be able to stand it, and you'd start skipping meals."

My mouth hangs open. "You noticed that?" That was early in our working relationship. I was saving all my money, afraid the job wouldn't last. That I wouldn't make the cut.

"Of course, I noticed. If a woman is gagging in front of me, I'd like it to be on purpose."

There's a challenging glint in his eyes, but I'm still caught up in the memory of those lentil soup days. They ended when he ordered Johann to make extra meals for me. *I need you in fighting form, not fainting from hunger,* he said to me. *That way, I can work you harder.* He had a little growl in his voice when he said, *Work you harder,* and I got so turned on I had to escape to a deserted conference room to have a little lie down.

I feel like I need a little lie down right now. My cheeks are flushed from the alcohol, and my thoughts are all over the place.

Was the private chef thing just his way of keeping me around?

No. He probably would've found it inconvenient if I fainted. I can imagine him stepping over my unconscious body on his way to his next meeting. The mental image reminds me of my rage.

"If I do run out of money, I can just get another job."

He stiffens. "Where?"

"All Cap would take me." I have no intention of working for another demanding boss, but this will piss Piers off. "I could work for Bryan."

"Brian with an 'I'?" Storm clouds gather on his brow. He doesn't just look pissed. He looks furious.

Tread cautiously, a part of me warns. The rest of me wants to pour whiskey on this dumpster fire. "Bryan with a 'Y.' But I bet either Brian would have me." I keep my tone cheerful, but when I remember Brian checking me out at a shareholder meeting, I have to suppress a shudder.

I'm just pretending to annoy Piers. But the way his face is turning red, I may have gone too far.

CHAPTER 3

"*Y*ou will go work for Brian with an 'I' over my dead body." He snatches the drink right out of my hand.

"What do you have against Brian with an 'I'?"

"He wants you."

"Why do you care?" It's not like I ever date anyone. I don't have the time.

Just this Tuesday, I got a surprise text from the captain of the Thrusters, asking me to be his date to the New Year's party, but I turned him down.

"I don't know why he asked me," I told Sloan, who was waiting for a meeting with the Dread Lord.

"Girl, you've had a glow up. All the footballers are gagging over you. Remember when Rinaldo asked if you'd be watching the field for him, and you said yes?"

"I was just being nice! I didn't know that was flirting."

"Okay, killer."

I told her I work too much to date. Every time I even think of going out, the Dread Lord manages to get invited to some yacht party or gala opening and needs me at his side to read people or remind him of their names.

"It would like Piers to be a dog in the manager," Sloan said.

I had to look that phrase up. It means he doesn't want me but doesn't want anyone else to have me, either. I thought Sloan was joking, but now I think she was right. She's VP of Sales, so she's even better at reading people than me.

"I'm not going to work for All Cap," I say. "Brian is gross."

"Which Brian?"

"Both of them. I'm done with having a boss."

"So what's the plan if you run out of money?"

"I'll figure it out."

"You could reel in a rich husband."

I snort and gesture to myself. "Do I look like trophy wife material?"

He says nothing, just looks at me in his intense way. Like he's seeing me, the real me, and he likes what he sees.

Sweet Santa, I wish that were true, but it's not. He just wants to make me squirm.

Why am I even trying to have a conversation with him? I'm day-drinking for the first time. Enjoying my new freedom, that's the task at hand.

"Give me my drink back."

"No."

I try to grab his arm and end up wrestling with him. He spins me around, clamping me against his body. He's so much bigger than me, it's not a fair fight. I wish I were wearing my red boots so I could stab his foot with my heel.

My body, already flooded with feelings, gets confused and thinks it's the start of sexy time. My breasts swell, and my pulse picks up, pounding between my legs. I'm weak with desire, which sucks because I'm supposed to be pummelling Piers, not swooning in his arms.

While I'm struggling to get free, he raises my glass to his lips.

"No!" I shout.

But it's too late. He chugs the creamy, light brown liquid, the muscles of his throat working in a smooth movement.

Baileys. He hates Baileys. And he's lactose intolerant.

"Ah, disgusting." He grabs the highball of whiskey and uses it to wash out his mouth.

"Why?" I cry. "Why would you do this?" First, he took away Christmas, so I turned to whiskey, and then he took that, too!

"You're acting ridiculous." His color is high, but his voice is sharp as ever. He can hold his liquor. I've never seen him affected by it.

Except that one night. But I vowed to myself to forget that night.

"Let me go." I kick at his shin until he does. I put a few feet between us and gesture to the liquor cabinet. "One thing. You couldn't let me have this one thing?"

"You're not thinking clearly."

"Oh, I'm thinking clearly." My voice is a little slurred, but I soldier on. "I'm thinking more clearly than I ever have."

Piers swallows. He half turns away and rests a hand over his stomach. The lactose must be hitting him.

"You need to take your pill," I mutter. "It's upstairs in my bag." I'm mad at him, but I don't want him in needless discomfort. Unless I decide to punch him in the stomach.

"I'm all right," he murmurs. "Thank you."

When he turns to me again, he hits me with the full blast of his charm. "You can't quit Wellesley." His tone is soft. Persuading. "Who will take care of me?"

My heart soars. He noticed! He noticed I take care of him.

"Who will entertain me during long meetings? Keep me

company in my cavernous office? Comfort me when the Fed raises rates?"

The picture he's painting of me is almost sweet. Almost.

He's just trying to keep me under his thumb. I used to love being made to feel small by him, but… I've outgrown that.

"You don't need me." It hurts, but I'm going to remind him of the woman he wants. "You have Scary Sandra."

His brows rise. "Scary Sandra?"

Oops. I didn't mean to call her that out loud. "Your 'consultant.'" I put air quotes around consultant. That's what she's called on his calendar, but I know better.

He blinks, like he doesn't know who I'm talking about. And isn't it just like him to forget the beautiful woman he's been seeing since September?

"Tall, blonde, wears a lot of red?" She looks like a sexy librarian crossed with a dominatrix. I can't really see Piers tolerating someone else taking charge, but I wonder… "You've had weekly meetings with her for the past four months." *Since Marty's funeral.* "I assume you're banging her."

"Sandra." Recognition dawns on his face, and then he looks like he's about to laugh.

My heart sinks to my socks. "Yeah. She can comfort you."

"Is this why you want to quit?" His soft tone is so unexpected, it makes me catch my breath. "You're jealous of Sandra?"

"What? No, I'm not jealous." I am totally jealous. "Why would I be jealous?"

"I am not banging Sandra." He puts a finger under my chin. "Wellesley, look at me."

I don't look at him. I look anywhere but at him. "No." A sigh shudders out of me, but then I harden my voice. "I'm quitting because I deserve better than you."

His hand falls away. I stare at the liquor cabinet so I can

get through my little speech. "You didn't need to drag me up here for work. You knew this holiday was important to me because of my mom. But you made sure I was trapped up here. With you. To be miserable. I'm done putting you first. I've done that these past few years and…" I bite back the rest: *Nothing's going to change.*

You'll never see the real me.

I want you to see the real me.

"I need to prioritize myself. Protect myself. It's clear you're never going to do that. You don't respect people. At this point, I don't think you're capable of it."

He doesn't say anything. His silence says it all.

Did I go too far? No, I could say much worse. *Your parents were jerks and fucked you up beyond repair. But it's okay, you have your money to keep you warm.*

Let Scary Sandra make sure you take your Lactase pill.

I don't say any of that. But I don't give in, either.

I let the silence stretch, and finally, he moves away. His slow footsteps recede until his brogues reach the carpet. He shuts the door.

There it is. I knew he would leave. He's going back to his stock tickers and end-of-the-year reports, where he belongs.

There's no reason for me to feel like I've broken something beyond repair.

By eleven, I have a taste for whiskey. The more I drink, the less gross it tastes!

Whiskey makes everything better. Whiskey understands.

After Piers left me alone, I went upstairs and dealt with some unfinished business. I emailed Johann and Benji, Pier's private chef and personal trainer, letting them know their future point of contact would no longer be me, but their schedule shouldn't change for the rest of the year. I also sent a staff-wide email doubling the bonuses of everyone in the company. I should email Sandra, too, but I decide Piers can deal with her himself.

Before I lost my nerve, I ran a bath and drowned my phone and iPad. I'll probably regret it, but in the moment, it felt good.

I officially have no job. I'm free!

I find the sound system and figure out how to change all the TVs to a channel that replays "It's A Wonderful Life" over and over again. Once that was playing on every screen, I turned on the house speakers and started blasting Christmas carols through the entire mansion.

I'd like to see him Bah Humbug his way out of this.

Now I'm in the home spa, sitting in the hot tub, wearing nothing but a Santa hat and singing, *Deck the halls with la la lolly.* I don't remember the words to this carol, but it doesn't matter as long as I shout the *fa la las.* Which I do. With gusto.

The hot tub was built into an alcove surrounded by more picture windows. I toast the mountains and gray sky and the clouds that are spitting snow again. We're going to be stuck here for a while. But it doesn't matter! Nothing matters!

The spa is on the lowest level of this ten-thousand-square-foot house. I can hibernate down here. Sleep on the massage bed next to the sauna. I doubt the Dread Lord and I will ever cross paths again.

I never have to see him again.

And if I feel a little sad about that, it's only because I haven't had enough to drink!

I'll miss him, though. Not just the perks of the job but seeing him every day.

I'll miss his pretty face. And the way he says "Wellesley" in that stern voice. Is that what he's like in bed? Deliciously strict and stern?

Crap, now I'm horny.

Not that I actually want to be in bed with my boss. Former boss. No, I'm just a normal, healthy woman whose libido is raging because she hasn't gotten laid in years.

I'm going to have to start fantasizing about someone else. It's possible I never wanted Piers; I just need to imagine someone saying mean things in a British accent to get off. Lots of people probably have that kink.

I can find porn I like instead. Or change it up and imagine a footballer instead.

But when my imagination starts flowing, it's still a tall, dark, and handsome boss chastising his assistant.

Enough of this impertinence, he clips, his plummy accent as sharp and as sparkling as Waterford crystal. *Hands on the desk and bend over.*

Crap, now I'm panting. My boobs are swollen and tender, and the insistent throbbing between my legs means my pussy is demanding an orgasm.

I distract myself with the high-tech panel on the side of the hot tub. I press some buttons, and the jets roar to life.

Which gives me an idea. What if I just sidle up to one of these gushing jets and open my legs? I just need the right angle...

But when I try it, the pressure leaves me gasping. It's like being fucked by a waterfall. Too much. My clit can't stand the deluge.

I turn back around, and the jet pummels my backside, which gives me an idea. If I just rise up and bend over so the jet stream hits between my butt cheeks... *Hmmm, that's nice.* Intense but nice.

My orgasm is building when the music blasting through the house cuts off. Piers must have found the electronics cabinet. He'll be stalking around the house, growling under his breath. He's so sexy when he's ready to go to war.

No, don't think of him! Definitely don't think about Fantasy No. Sixty Nine, where he's pulling my hair, whispering, *Bad, bad girl—*

All the jets in the hot tub die. "Dammit!" I scramble to push the button again but freeze when I hear footsteps on the stairs.

I hope I've imagined it, but no, it's the Dread Lord, here to spoil my fun. He would show up just as I figured out how to get the fancy hot tub to stimulate my butthole.

I open my mouth to give him a piece of my mind.

But when he walks in, he looks like he hasn't slept in a year.

He's sexy as ever, but I spot the signs of dishevelment. His shirt has a few wrinkles. The shadows under his eyes are deeper, darker. His hair is tousled like he's run his hand through it more than once. In all my years of observing him, that's something he's never done.

Seeing these signs of humanity softens me. It's like the time I found an old photo of him as a boy, in a little holiday suit complete with plaid vest and bowtie. He looked adorable, but there was a sadness in his golden eyes. He looked a little lost.

He had that same lost expression after Marty's funeral.

I know what it's like to lose someone who's your whole world. It changes you.

It changed Piers. But not enough.

Now, though, he looks terrible. He's missing a cufflink. For anyone else, that's not a big deal, but for the owner of a multinational conglomerate that includes several luxury brands and fashion houses? He's on the brink of devastation.

Is it the dairy? There was no way I could've made him take a lactose pill before he drank my drink, but I still feel guilty. Responsible.

No, don't feel sorry for him. Harden your heart.

Dear Santa,

Make me as black-hearted as him!

He prowls toward me, a pout on his perfect lips. He still looks hot, but maybe that's just because my butthole is still tingling.

"That's a two-hundred-thousand-dollar bottle of scotch," he says.

"I know," I hiccup. "Your favorite. I've always wanted to taste it."

"You have tasted it." His eyes glow. "Remember?"

Oh no, he didn't. He didn't just bring up that night. We never talk about that night.

I'm saved when he changes the subject. "Have you eaten?"

"Does the Baileys count as breakfast?"

"No."

"Then nope."

"Put the bottle down," he orders, and my breathing grows heavy as my pussy throbs. I love it when he gets stern.

"Make me."

His nostrils flare as he inhales. I've always found his nostril flares to be incredibly sexy.

"Give it to me." He holds out a hand.

I set the bottle to my lips. "You want it, come take it."

Another nostril flare. I squeeze my thighs together.

I see the moment he makes his decision. He looks stone-faced, almost resigned. But then a mischievous light enters his eyes.

Oh no. I only see that look of victory when he's decimated his enemies. Bankrupted a rival.

He starts undoing the buttons of his shirt.

"What are you doing?"

He removes his remaining cufflink and strips off his button-down shirt. He's wearing an undershirt, but the thin cotton does nothing to disguise the taut muscles underneath. His arms are so defined, and he has corded veins.

Corded veins!

"I'm doing as you instructed." He toes off his left brogue, then the other. "I'm making you." He strips off his socks before his hands go to his belt.

"Wait," I cry. I'm out of breath, and I have this feeling that if he continues stripping, something dreadful will happen, but the rest of my body is celebrating. *This is even better than Fantasy No. Sixty Nine!*

He holds my gaze the whole time he takes off his pants. "You know, you're right."

I blink at him. He's standing in front of me in an undershirt and boxer briefs that show off his muscular limbs. Dark hair dusts his thighs.

I've waited years for him to admit I'm right, but now that it's here, I can't focus on enjoying it. I can't focus on anything but the bunched muscles of his shoulders or the sculpted quads. He looks so slim underneath his suits!

Santa, save me.

I lick my lips. "What was I right about?" I can barely get the words out. He's looking at me like he's a bull and I'm a red flag.

"If I want something, I take it."

I don't think he's talking about the whiskey. My pussy pulses, and I can't stop my whimper. I want to be taken. I want to be taken so bad!

"You're going to start acting sensible," he says. "No more drinking, your cheeks are flushed. And you need to eat something."

My whole body is flushed, but not just because of the hot tub.

He walks towards me, still lecturing. I need to drink more water, blah blah blah. "You've had your fun. You're going to take a little nap and wake up fresh for the night's work. You're going to drop this nonsense about quitting. I'm willing to overlook your impertinence—"

"Excuse me?" I can't believe him. The arrogance of this man! "I'm quitting, and there's nothing you can do about it." I lift the bottle and start chugging.

It doesn't work; I can't get much down before I cough and sputter. I'm pretty bad at being a bad girl, but it doesn't matter. I just need practice.

If it's possible, his glare turns even more frigid. I shiver even though I'm in water heated to over a hundred degrees Fahrenheit.

"Enough," he snaps. "Put the bottle down."

This is another power play. He doesn't want the whiskey; he just can't stand to let me enjoy myself. He wants to ruin my fun.

He doesn't get to do that anymore.

I stand straight up. Water streams off of me as I point the mouth of the bottle at myself. "You're not the boss of me."

Then I remember… I'm naked.

CHAPTER 4

"Omigod!" I drop back into the water so fast, I forget that I'm holding the bottle. I lift it quickly, but it's too late. The whiskey has been tainted with chlorine. Oh well. I set the bottle on the side of the hot tub.

I have more pressing things to deal with.

Namely, the fact that my boss just saw my bare naked body. I could've worn my bra and thong, but I've never skinny dipped in a hot tub in a ten-thousand-square-foot mountain chalet. It seemed like a great way to start my retirement.

I think I might be drunk.

The Dread Lord is staring at me. His eyes are glowing as usual, but his pupils are so wide they've turned his eyes black. The gold is only a thin corona around them. His throat works as he swallows.

He pulls his undershirt over his head.

Holy hell. I nearly fall backward into the hot tub because he's gorgeous. I thought his arms were chiseled, but his abdomen is a work of art. And he's packing plenty of inches in those tight, black briefs.

No, don't look at his dick! His giant, throbbing meat stick... Don't even think of it!

"Like what you see?" He's suddenly next to the hot tub. Right beside me. I could reach out and touch his eight-pack.

"Benji really works you hard." Benji is the only one who can yell at the Dread Lord and survive. Sometimes, I listen in on their workouts because the sound of a former SEAL team instructor barking at my boss gives me so much joy. I only got the soundtrack, though, no visuals.

"Did you think that Benji and I were having tea?"

"No, just lots of sex." I mimic Benji's Brooklyn accent. "Yeah, that's good. Give it to me again. Come on now, one more time, yeah, yeah, pump it like you mean it."

A muscle jerks in his cheek, but the corner of his mouth is turning up, like he's fighting a smile. "Glad we could amuse you."

"It's one of the things I'm going to miss. That and spitting into your espresso." I have never spat in his espresso.

His eyes narrow. "You've been very naughty."

I gasp like he's put his hands on me. His words shoot straight to my needy clit.

"An absolute disgrace." He puts a hand on the side of the hot tub. It's large and strong and dusted with black hair, and all I can think about is how it would feel if he touched me.

He heaves himself into the water. I retreat until my back hits the side of the hot tub and squeak as he advances on me. The huge hot tub is suddenly not big enough for the two of us. He's everywhere, with his rock-hard chest and boulders in his shoulders.

He grabs me, moving so fast I don't have time to shriek.

His hand fists in my hair, drawing my head back. It stings in a way that makes me want more. "What are you going to do to me?"

"What I should've done a long time ago." He lowers his head

and stifles my gasp with a kiss. Those perfect lips claim mine, and I automatically press into him, even though he's holding my head back by my hair, hard enough to hurt. I rub myself against his body, and little electrical pulses run through me.

I have never been kissed like this before. I'm in a fever dream. He's kissing me like he's going to suck all the whiskey from me, and I moan when I shift my hips and feel his hard length.

"You're a bad, bad girl." He takes a break from mauling my mouth to nip at my jaw. Lightning shoots down my legs, and I collapse. He shifts us so that he's sitting and I'm on top of him.

I grind down, chasing more of that lightning. I'm so close to coming, I'm going to bite him if I don't get it soon. "The worst. Absolutely incorrigible." He bares his teeth at me. His hair is mussed, wild. "The way you tempt me, Wellesley."

What?

"The things you do to me." He hauls me up by my hair so now I'm kneeling, straddling him. My body bows backward, pushing my breasts toward him. "Slipping your bra off in the middle of a work night."

"You noticed that?"

His groan reverberates through me and makes my inner muscles spasm with ecstasy. "I couldn't notice anything else. These tantalizing little nipples." He leans in and licks one, then bites it. The pain sizzles through me, my orgasm rising. "I wanted to bend you over right there and punish you for tempting me—"

My orgasm slams into me like a train. "Oh god," I shout to the ceiling. "Oh fuck."

"Yes, that's it. Give it to me." He pulls me close, loosening his grip just enough that I can rub my pussy against the ridge of his cock.

"You're so hard," I moan.

"All for you, Wellesley, all for you." He still has that punishing grip on my hair—pain pulses through my scalp, adding to the maelstrom of feeling—but now he's forcing me close. Right where I want to be.

I writhe against him, in the grip of a sudden storm of pleasure.

I rub one out every night fantasizing about him. Let's be honest, it was always him, not a faceless man. But last night I passed out before my nightly orgasm, so now I'm riding high on a twenty-four-hour backlog of desire.

And here he is, with his powerful body and movie star eyes, and it doesn't seem real.

"Wellesley." He says my name like I'm his salvation. For a moment, I'm floating above the clouds.

I lick my Piers-bitten lips. My mind is clearing. I'm in my boss's lap, naked, and I just used his abs like a sexy washboard to scrub my clit. I feel sexy and beautiful, but… am I? Is this really happening?

Is this really me?

"Holy hell." My limbs are weak, but I push at him, trying to put some distance between us. "What was that?"

"You know what that was. And it was glorious." He looks so satisfied, it's distracting.

What was I trying to say? "We can't do this."

"Why not?"

"You're my boss!"

"You quit, remember?"

"You didn't accept my resignation." I push at him again, but he grips my hips, settling me more firmly and straddling his lap. His cock is still hard, and, Sweet St. Nick, I want all that pastrami in my mouth.

He's looking at me like I'm the sexiest thing he's ever

seen. His fingers caress my hips, and sensation shoots through me, making my nipples tingle.

"We can't do this. What about—" I gulp. A chill trickles through me when I realize what I've just done. "What about Scary Sandra?"

"What about her?"

"She's your..." I falter before saying *girlfriend.* I don't know if Piers dates people. Once, in his early twenties, he was photographed out to dinner with every underwear model from the Victoria's Secret spring catalog—all twenty-four of them at one long table—but I don't know if that counts as dating. I do know that he hasn't gone out with anyone since I started working for him. "You're banging her."

"I'm not banging her."

I shake my head in horror. What have I done? I'm the other woman... I'm the worst.

"I'm not," Piers shakes me. "I swear it on Marty's grave."

The pressure in my skull pops, leaving me limp with relief. He wouldn't say that if he didn't mean it. He never mentions Marty if he can help it.

"What if I told you I haven't been intimate with anyone in almost five years?"

"What? Why?" My world wobbles on its axis.

"Wellesley," his voice turns warm. "Are you really asking me that?" He's looking at me with such tenderness, it can't be real.

Does scotch cause hallucinations?

"Four years, eleven months, and twenty-seven days I've been waiting for this," he murmurs. "I just didn't know it."

Four years... That's when he hired me. The day we met. I'd impressed him with intel about his competitors, and he hired me on the spot.

Does he mean he's wanted to bang me? From day one?

It's too much for me to believe. I keep shaking my head.

He stops me with another kiss. "It's better than I imagined."

What little strength I've gained in the past minute leaves my body, and I collapse against him. My boss has imagined kissing me?

"Is it so hard to believe?" He traces a finger along my collarbone.

"Oh god," I whimper.

"You can call me Piers. 'Milord,' if you're feeling medieval."

I hide my face in my hands, and he chuckles.

"I always thought the Dread Lord was a mouthful." He lifts my wet hair off my shoulder and drops his head to press his lips to my skin. "That's what people call me, right?"

"Yes." My answer is muffled by my palms.

"It's okay, I like it. And that one time you called me 'sir' in an email, I had to jack off for an hour."

His cock is hard under my butt, so... he's not lying.

I whimper. I can't deal.

"Enough." He pecks me on the forehead. "Let's get you out of this hell broth." He lifts me in his arms. I feel so small and perfect, cradled against him. He carries me out of the hot tub, wraps me with a towel warmed on the rack, and draws me down to settle in his lap again, this time on the couch. His cock is still hard, and I keep wondering what's next. But then my brain glitches out.

My boss wants me. He's always wanted me. Not Scary Sandra. Me. ????? That's where my brain keeps glitching.

He grabs a bottle of water from the side table and opens it.

"Drink." He sets the bottle to my lips. He doesn't let me take it from him, just holds it for me, giving me small sips until I've had half the bottle. And I'd be lying if I said that his controlling behavior didn't make me weak. "More?"

I shake my head.

"Good girl."

I've wanted to hear those words from him for so long, and they sound better than I imagined. I melt. My limbs are boneless when he shifts me onto the couch and tucks another towel around me. "Now don't move." He stands up and heads to the sauna room, presumably to get us two robes.

It takes a second for me to figure out how to use my legs, and when I do, I'm as wobbly as a new colt. But I make a break for it. I don't know what the Dread Lord is up to, and I have no power to resist him. I need to escape!

He catches me before I get to the stairs.

And that's how I find myself tossed over his shoulder and carried upstairs like a sack of grain.

"Put me down!" I kick my legs, and he claps a hand to my ass. Not hard, but he has a big hand, and any more force and it would sting.

"No. I told you not to move, and you disobeyed me. Bad girl." His voice has the perfect amount of growl to it, and his hand rubs my bottom, soothing me. He's the Dread Lord of all my fantasies come to life. But not even Fantasies Number One through Seven Thousand, Six Hundred and Twelve prepared me for how I respond to him. If he sets me down, I'd fall to my knees and beg for his cruelty. There's no way I can fight him.

So I give up, going limp and letting my head and wet hair hang down to the floor.

He carries me through the house, up to the top floor. From my upside-down position, it takes me a moment to recognize my bedroom. He carries me into the bathroom, right into the shower and leaves me dangling while he turns on the warm spray.

Finally, he sets me down. "Let's get you clean so I can dirty you up again."

Santa, save me!

The shower is one of those fancy glass-enclosed ones. It's enormous, with a stone bench for sitting, but no amount of space is enough because the Dread Lord is in the shower with me. Not only is he hanging around, but he takes the hand sprayer down and uses it to rinse me off. I turn to grab it away from him, and he flips me around so my back is to his front. His dick pokes me, but he clamps his arm around me so I'm trapped.

And then he directs the spray between my legs. I cry out, writhing, trying to get away, but he holds me tight and uses the jet right above my clit. It really is like being fucked by a waterfall.

Sweet Santa, I thought I had elaborate Dread Lord fantasies, but I never imagined this. This blows even Fantasy No. Sixty-nine away.

It's not just the pressure pummelling my sexy bits. It's also Piers, his muscles bunching as he grips my neck and holds me fast, making me take it. He knows just how to direct the sprayer, too, so it doesn't hit my clit directly. Not too much, just enough to drown me in pleasure. My muscles clench, cramp, and release. Did I come? I think I just came again.

Piers's cock is a club in my back, a promise. A threat. But he's ignoring his own needs, still pummelling me with the spray, driving me toward a third climax.

"Oh my god," I whimper. "Oh my god."

"I told you, darling, you can call me 'Piers.' Or Milord if you're feeling medieval."

I laugh despite myself. "Shut up."

"Oh no, you don't." He maneuvers me to the wall and

presses me against the tile. "You don't tell me what to do. I'm still in charge." Too late, I realize there are more jets built into the wall. Now, I'm caught between Piers and a hard spray. I try to fold in half, to see if I can slip away, but he clamps a hand on the back of my neck and keeps me pinned, cheek to the tile. The spray batters my clit. I scrabble at the slick marble, and he presses harder into my back. "Be still. You can't escape me."

Oh fuck, I'm going to come again. My poor battered clit is tender, overstimulated. But my pussy throbs, and my insides ache, needing to be filled.

"Please," I beg. "Please fuck me."

A sharp inhale.

"Not yet. You have to earn that, my sweet Wellesley."

I whimper. He sounds like all of my fantasies rolled into one.

"Now be a good girl and reach back. Hold your ass open for me."

He's not going to show me mercy. My breath hitches on a sob, but I do as I'm told and reach back, parting my ass cheeks so he can direct the spray onto the tender pleats of my asshole. He teases me, circling my rear hole, getting closer and backing off, until I'm shaking. My fingers are slipping on my wet skin, and my face is smushed to the tile, but I don't want him to let up and let me go, never, never, never. I want it all, and I want him to make me take it.

"That's a good girl," he purrs, as he punishes me with pleasure. I come again with a white hot, supernova blast.

CHAPTER 5

I'm pretty sure I passed out, because when I come to, I'm cradled in Piers's arms. The water's off, and he's sitting on the bench, holding me in his lap. My mouth is lax, and I close it quickly so I don't drool.

I let him dry me off. He fusses over me, rubbing a small towel over my scalp. "Your hair."

"It's unmanageable."

"Like you." He presses a kiss to my temple and rubs the towel over my chest. I don't know if it's on purpose, but the movement teases my nipples. My pussy gives a sad little pulse. It feels empty.

"You didn't fuck me." The whiskey and the orgasms removed my filter. I can't keep my thoughts from tumbling out of my mouth if I tried. I'm exposed, swathed in fluffy white towels, but still naked in his lap.

"I will." Another kiss and he lifts me in his arms. "All in due time."

He sets me on the bed. "Get dressed. Unless you want me to help you?"

"I can dress myself." I scramble to catch the towel before

it falls and press it to my chest, covering my bare boobs. I'm feeling very vulnerable right now.

And Piers looks like he always has. Fierce and in control.

For a moment, his expression softens. "Don't try to fight this, Wellesley. There's nowhere to run. I'm going to get you fed and sobered up, and then we're going to talk."

"What are we going to talk about?"

"That night, for starters. Get dressed. I'm going to get some food. What are you in the mood to eat?"

He turns around, and I can't look anywhere but his black briefs. I've never seen him in anything less than a suit. And now all those pretty muscles are on display, and his cock is tenting the sodden fabric.

"Wellesley? Are you craving anything to eat?"

"Pastrami," I say, before thinking. Once I register what I've said, my eyes go wide, but it's too late to take it back.

"Noted." He smirks.

"I meant to say meat. You know, protein. Can't get enough protein. It's good for you." I'm babbling. I shut my mouth and give him a thumbs up. It doesn't seem enough, so I put up a second thumb. Double thumbs!

He shakes his head. "Just how much did you have to drink?"

I don't have to answer because he exits after asking that question, closing the door behind him.

I could run. But where would I go? I'm trapped in this mansion. My hair would freeze before I took two steps outside.

Even if I did try to run, he's made it clear he'll chase me.

Shiver. Suddenly, I have a whole new index of fantasies to be filed under *Primal Piers*.

By the time Piers returns, not only am I dressed, but I'm swathed in the thickest, ugliest sweater I brought.

He walks in, carrying the entire Nantucket pie on a

marble cake pedestal. Bare-chested, in loose gray pajama pants, he's the hottest thing I've ever seen. Beyond every fantasy.

This is Saturday morning Piers. Lazy holiday Piers. He looks so good, I ache.

He's still Piers, though, so his gaze sharpens when he catches sight of me in my oversized fleece sweater monstrosity. It's holiday-themed and covered in kitten heads. The kittens are wearing Santa hats, because Christmas.

Piers glowers at the kittens like he's just learned they committed hate crimes. "What are you wearing?"

"Like it?" I raise my arms, which are draped in fabric that extends six inches past my fingertips. I could fit a whole other one of me under here, plus the cake stand. Which is good, because it'll hide my food baby after I eat that entire pie. "It's a HoodZou. You don't know what a HoodZou is?"

He settles next to me on the bed and secures the cake stand between us. My stomach growls as he hands me a fork. "Enlighten me."

"It's a cross between a hoodie and a mumu. The most comfortable thing you'll ever wear, guaranteed."

His lip curls. "It should be burned."

"You wouldn't dare." I point a fork at him. "I love this thing. Now that I'm retired, I'm going to wear it nonstop."

"Looks a bit warm for Addis Ababa."

My mouth falls open. "How did you figure it out?"

"You have all these travel blogs bookmarked in your browser. I did some snooping after you tendered your resignation." He passes a hand over his face. He still looks tired. He probably only slept a few hours last night. He likes to live on China Standard time. The trouble is, he also likes to live on Eastern Standard Time and Greenwich Mean Time, too.

I dig into the pie. Piers is quiet, like he needs a break from talking. His shoulders slope a little, and lines are bracketing his mouth. I study them while I eat.

"How long have you been planning to escape me?" he asks.

"I…" I stop. I don't want to lie. "From the beginning. But it wasn't an escape. I never thought I'd last this long in the job."

"Why not?"

Is he really asking that? "Because I'd make a mistake and you'd fire me."

"Am I such an ogre?" His face is carefully blank. Is he upset?

I open my mouth. Close it.

He looks away. "Never mind. You don't have to answer."

Did I hurt his feelings? I didn't know he had feelings to hurt.

I cover his hand with mine, and his head snaps back to me. I don't know what to say, though, so I fork a piece of pie and hold it up. "I don't know what this is, but I think you might like it." He leans in to taste it, but I pull the fork back. "It has dairy. You need to take your pill. In my purse." I wait until he's dug out the Lactase bottle and swallowed a pill, then feed him bites of the pie. We both agree that the texture is more like cake.

"Thank you for taking care of me," he says in a rare show of appreciation.

"You're welcome." He has loads of people catering to his every whim. But who really knows him? "I don't think you're an ogre."

"Yes, you do."

"You're confusing me with Sloan. And everyone else in the office."

He's not rude, I once defended him to Sloan. *It's just his dry wit. He's actually hilarious.*

He's not, she told me. *You're just uniquely equipped to handle him. God help us all when you realize you deserve better.*

He gives a bitter laugh. "They think I'm the worst."

"You're not the worst, you're just British. Upper crust. Keep a stiff upper lip, guv-nor!" I try for an Eliza Doolittle accent.

"Never do that again."

"You're not the boss of me." I lick my fork clean.

"Was it really so terrible working for me?" He sounds like he doesn't care, but I sense that he does. He cares a ton.

"No. The perks were nice. I am going to miss the perks." I'm not going to give in and tell him I loved working with him. His snark, his intensity. The long work hours watching his brilliant mind take on the toughest business problems.

I can't tell him I'll miss him. The highs and lows, the rollercoaster. The giddiness I felt when I walked into his office early Monday morning.

I can't risk it.

I have to guard my heart.

"Jetting to Tokyo. Eating at five Michelin-starred restaurants in three days. Front row seats at Milan Fashion Week. Owner's box at the Thrusters game. They were my mother's favorite soccer team, you know."

"I know." His golden gaze is fixed on me, unblinking. "Is that all?"

I shake my head, refusing to give him an answer. "Will you miss me?"

"Yes." He answers instantly. I'm shocked he's sharing so openly. He usually keeps his cards close to his chest. "But will you miss me? I want to know."

I cross my arms over my chest. I'm getting overheated in my Houdzou, but I'm not taking it off. I need all the armor I can get. I want to answer, but I need to protect myself. He's not hiding anymore, but I am.

He grips my ankle. It's an innocuous touch that has me swallowing hard and pressing my legs together because I don't think my panties will keep me from leaking on the sheets.

"What can I say to get you to tell me the truth?"

I raise my chin. "Tell me who Sandra is."

He sighs. I can see the walls coming back up, and my heart sinks. But then he says, "She's my therapist."

"What?" I drop the fork.

Piers retrieves it. It's already spotless, but he cleans it off in his mouth. My inner muscles clench at the sight.

"Therapy? You've been in therapy?"

"Since Marty…" His Adam's apple bobs. My normally stoic boss looks away, his expression suddenly lost. It's the most human I've seen him. And it's the same expression he wore as a child, in the photo of him I found. The one he told me to throw away.

"Sandra's your therapist," I repeat. I can't believe it.

"She is. Once a week for two hours." He huffs. "She gets me to feel my feelings."

I gasp.

"I know, I have feelings outside of greed and avarice. It was a shock to me, too."

I fumble for his hand. "Don't do that. Don't put yourself down before anyone else can." *The way your parents did.* "Of course you have feelings, you're human. Men often get socialized not to show anything but rage, but they still feel all those emotions."

"You sound like Sandra," he mutters.

Something unclenches in my chest. "Therapy. Who knew." I want to laugh, I feel so light. Piers in therapy is a goddamn Christmas miracle.

Maybe there is something in him worth redeeming. Maybe deep down, there's a lost little boy who just needs love. But haven't I always known that?

I still have the photograph. I didn't throw it away; I hid it in my wallet. Whenever Piers was being particularly insufferable, I'd pull the photo out and imagine him as that boy. It made me a little kinder. I vowed to be a ray of sunshine in his gloomy life. I choose to see the best in him, at every turn.

Until this morning, when I gave up on him. I thought I'd have to give up on him for good, but maybe…

"It's helping. And I needed it. No man is an island, no matter how much I want to be. And after Marty passed…" His expression is pained. Here's more proof that Piers is human: he's still grieving his business partner. "He was alone, you know. At the end."

"I know," I say softly. "But he wasn't alone. He had you."

"He did. I spent the last few holidays with him, you know. His own children couldn't stand him. Probably because he was divorcing wife number six, and she was younger than all of them."

"He had terrible taste in women." I have to grin, because Marty always joked about it.

"I would agree, except he always thought the world of you. Told me I was the luckiest man in the world to have you by my side." He opens his mouth like he's going to say more, then hesitates.

"He thought the world of you, too," I say.

"He did, God knows why. He bet on me. Put his money behind me."

"He believed in you."

"More than my own father did." He licks his lips. "Wellesley, I… we need to talk about that night."

That night. The night of the funeral.

"I remember." Piers and I were in Marty's home office, presumably to pack up some of his final documents. Piers found a bottle of scotch in a drawer. *Marty outbid the Brians at All Cap for this. Couldn't wait to drink it.*

He drank half the bottle himself. He looked so devastated, so alone, and I felt his hurt like my own pain. I went to him, took the bottle out of his hands, and helped him drink the rest.

"Do you?"

"Sorta." I wrinkle my nose. I remember the scotch burned in my throat, but the fire was nothing compared with wanting Piers. I wanted to be close to him. I wanted him to let me in. And suddenly the bottle was empty, and we were kissing. He kissed me so hard, he bent me backward over the desk. For a moment, I was ready for him to rip off my black tights and take me right on Marty's desk.

"Did you feel it?" he asks me now, his gaze molten on mine.

I duck my head. I can't look at him and confess this. "Yes," I whisper to the cats on my HoudZou.

He touches my chin with gentle fingers. "Wellesley."

I'm so tired of holding myself back. Of fighting to be apart from him. I hate the inches of air separating us. I can't stand them and want them gone. I want to lunge into his arms.

So I do.

The fork goes flying. The cake stand tips over. Gooey cranberries are getting everywhere, smearing red on the perfect white sheets, and I don't fucking care. I need him to hold me. Right now. I let my weight rest in the circle of his strong arms while our mouths meet. I might be crying. I might be laughing. I might be a messy puddle of emotions, but it doesn't matter because he's holding me together.

Do you feel it?

Yes. I feel it too.

"Finally," he growls. He clutches me to him, his hands

squeezing my arms like he's reassuring himself I'm real. His fingers clamp down, holding me for his kiss. I can't get away. I don't want to get away, but it's overwhelming, the feel of those perfect lips on mine.

I break away, panting. "I don't understand. I don't understand what's happening. We kissed, and then you pulled away. You never mentioned it again."

And Sandra walked into his office the next day.

Sandra, his therapist. Not his lover.

"I never should've kissed you like that."

"Oh." That hurts.

"Oh my darling." He cups the back of my head and pulls me close, and even though I'm stiff with hurt, I let him. I just love it when he calls me *darling*. "No, you misunderstand. Not because I didn't want to. Do you know what Marty told me, right before he died?"

"What?"

"I shouldn't tell you. You think I'm mad as it is."

Mad, as in crazy.

"I don't think you're mad. I don't know what to think." I realize I'm leaning a hand on his abs. I trace a finger over his happy trail. He's so beautiful, I ache. "You never let me in."

"I'm trying, Wellesley. Believe me."

I glance down at the bed, cranberries smashed and staining the coverlet red. "We made a mess."

He rips the coverlet out of its hospital corners and bundles up the mess, pushing it out of the way. He's covered the chaos with a pretty white blanket, but I know what's underneath.

He turns back to me and sees how I'm curled up, with my knees against my chest, in a HoudZou fortress. His face shutters.

"Are you all right?"

"I'm…" I don't know what to think. It's too late to run, but

I can still hide. I have to. If he knew how much I've fantasized about him, he would think I'm pathetic.

"Have I lost you forever, then?"

"I don't know." I wish I did. The smartest plan would be to escape him, but… I'm not going to escape my fantasies of what-could-of-been, even if I run all the way to Addis Ababa.

He kneels beside me on the bed. "You'll miss me."

I nod, my chin knocking against my knees.

"So let me in. Just this once. Let me make you feel good."

I don't want it to be just once. But this is Piers Lord. He doesn't do relationships. He'll get his orgasm and go.

But maybe I can fulfill a few of my fantasies before he does.

I slide my legs down the bed, unfolding a little. "I don't know what you want from me."

"Just you, Wellesley. Beautiful, perfect you."

"I'm not perfect."

"You are though, darling. Let me show you." His hand encircles my ankle. He's waiting for permission.

I should say no.

I should tell him to fuck off. I should scream and cry and let him know that I erected walls like his and buried myself behind them because of him.

I don't. I open my legs and give him a glimpse of paradise.

CHAPTER 6

*P*iers's eyes light when he looks between my legs, but then he frowns. "There's a cat on your panties."

"It's a pussy." I give him a wide smile. He won't want me forever, but he wants me now, and I'm going to enjoy it. "And you want to pet it, don't you?" I rock my hips, letting the Houdzou slide up further.

"Do not get fresh with me."

"You like it when I get fresh… *Sir.*"

His breath gusts out of him. Oh, he likes being called *Sir.*

"You like it when I'm naughty."

"I do, dirty girl. I do." He takes both ankles and pulls me down the bed. I let him, stretching my arms above my head. He pulls me flush against him, leaning in to kiss me. "I'm going to work you so hard," he murmurs against my mouth.

"Are you going to dress me down?"

"Mmm, yes."

"What if I get cold?"

"I'll keep you warm. I'll crank up the thermostat permanently, if it means you'll never wear that thing again."

I'm already wriggling out of my Houdzou, letting him whip it off of me.

"That's better. Arms over your head, let me see you."

I reach for the headboard, enjoying the way he gazes at my bare breasts. "Yes, milord."

"Cheeky peasant."

I arch my back, feeling so very wet.

Any minute now he's going to rip off my panties and plunge inside me. I can't wait.

But he's taking his sweet time. He lays on top of me, still in his pajama pants. I lift my hips, trying to rub against his groin. He kisses me again, and I groan into his mouth.

"Shh, let me enjoy this." His hands are everywhere, caressing my bare skin. I feel so beautiful, so cherished. All his intensity focused on me. It's the most addictive thing in the world, being the object of his desire.

Even if it won't last.

"I need you wet," he says. He crawls down my body and props my legs on his shoulders.

"I am wet." I'm panting at the sight of him like this.

He presses a kiss to my calf. "Not enough for me. For this." He nods to the bulge in his pants. I slide a foot down and press it against his length.

Fuck, there's a lot of him.

"Bad girl," he mutters as I stroke the arch of my foot over him. "Incurably naughty."

"What are you going to do about it?"

The next thing I know, he's flipped me to my belly and smacked my ass. "This." He hooks his fingers into the sides of my panties and rips them in two.

"Hey," I cry, craning my neck to look back at him. "Those are my panties."

He lifts them to his face and inhales my scent before tossing them away. "You won't be needing panties anymore."

I'm about to argue—I wear those every Christmas—but he props me up on my knees and thrusts two fingers into my sopping wet pussy.

"Oh god," I moan and get a mouthful of down pillow.

Another smack on my ass. "That's not what you call me."

I'm face down, my upper torso pressed to the bed while he finger fucks the shit out of me. I clench on his fingers, my climax building in my lower belly.

He stops when I'm close and smacks my ass again. Like I'm one of his prized cattle. "What do you call me?"

"You're a pain in my ass. Ow!"

He bit me!

"I'm going to be a pain in your ass. Would you like that?" He parts my ass cheeks and licks between them.

I can't answer. I'm vibrating, arching my back to push myself onto his tongue, drooling in the sheets.

"You don't have to tell me. You're dripping into my hand."

Tongue in my ass, fingers in my pussy. He teases me like that until I'm a naked bunch of nerves, endlessly tingling.

"That's it, dirty girl. Get nice and wet for me so I can fill you with my cock." He scrapes his teeth over my freshly spanked ass, drawing new shudders from me.

"You're so mean."

"You love it." He stops to put on a condom. The black and gold wrapper flutters to the floor, and then he's teasing me with the head of his dick, swirling it around in my wetness. "I'm a lot to take," he warns me.

Even with my face pressed into the pillow, I smile. "I know. But I can take you."

"You're the only one who can." And then he's pressing inside, filling me, and I can't think. There's no room for thoughts, or worries, or witty comebacks. There's only Piers.

"Oh my darling," he sighs as he strokes his hands down my back, my sides. Soothing me like a skiddish horse. He lets me wriggle and get used to his girth, my inner muscles kissing along his cock as I adjust to him.

But once he's wedged inside me, he can't help getting mean again. "There's a good girl." He grabs my wild hair and uses it like reins to pull my head back. Once my spine is bowed back, he slides all the way in. The air leaves my lungs. My fingers flex, looking for purchase on the mattress. "Easy." He gives a few experimental thrusts, and I panic. He's rearranging my guts but in a good way. This is going to ruin me for sex with anyone else, I can just tell.

"Take. It. All." He punches his hips into me, pulling my hair, and the sting is so delicious I come hard.

I give in and go limp, letting him ride me, then flip me over and pull me onto his lap so I can ride him. He grips my hips and guides them into a rocking motion. "That's it, beautiful. Ride me."

It's hard to breathe with his cock splitting me. With his incredible body stretched out below me, muscles rippling under my palms. But the way he's looking at me, I feel sexy and desired. He digs his fingers into my love handles like he's afraid I'll get away. I cup my breasts and stroke my nipples, giving him a show, and he looks like he's witnessing a miracle.

And when his gaze goes hazy, and he takes over, pounding into me from below until he cums? He's the most perfect thing I've ever seen.

My happiness is bittersweet. This was the best sex of my life. None of my fantasies can compare, which is too bad, because they'll be all I'll have when this is over.

* * *

IN THE MIDDLE of the night, my eyes pop open. Piers is asleep next to me, and we're in his bed because after sexy times in my bedroom, the entire bed was a wet spot.

I'm wide awake. My body is sore but in a good way.

The moon is shining through the windows. The sky is finally clear. But we're still snowed in, in our own little world.

I wish I could stay here, snuggled up with Piers, and enjoy the moment.

But I can't help feeling I'm on the precipice of something huge. One wrong step, and I'll lose everything.

Maybe I already have. Because what happens when the holiday ends? When Piers goes back to work, and I leave him, forever.

I don't want to think about it, but I have to. I pull away, easing carefully out of the bed. Piers' mouth twitches, but he remains still. He's on his stomach, his beautiful face turned toward me. Those long lashes leave shadows on his cheeks.

He must be exhausted after driving himself all week. All year. He needs to sleep. He looks so peaceful, though, I don't want to stop staring at him.

Who am I kidding? It doesn't matter where I go. How far I run. I'm never getting over Piers.

But I need to move. I get dressed and creep downstairs. Piers and I burned off all the calories from the Nantucket pie, so it's time for lasagna. I heat it up in the microwave and eat it straight out of the pan.

After food, I find myself back in front of the picture windows. The colorful glow of the lights on the fir tree bathes my face.

It's after midnight and officially December twenty-fifth. If I were home, I'd be clicking through TV channels, catching snatches of old holiday movies. I'd stay up late, hoping to sleep in the next day, knowing my only Christmas plans would be a trek to Rockefeller Center. Kinda pathetic, but I guess I've clung to the tradition because it made me feel close to my mom.

I don't know how long I stand there, wrapped in the quiet. I'm warm in my Houdzou and Christmas socks, and those quiet moments where the world is only lit by the lights on the tree have always been my favorite.

I stay long enough that I'm not surprised when I hear the creak of footsteps on the stairs. Piers must have woken and come looking for me.

I don't turn. I let him prowl to me to stand at my back. He comes close but doesn't touch me. I can feel him wanting to hold me but holding himself back.

"What are you thinking of?" he murmurs.

"It's Christmas."

"Do you wish you were home?"

"No." As I say it, I realize it's true.

His arms come around me. He kisses my hair and rests his chin on my head.

I relax back against him. Being in his arms feels right. "Why this Christmas? Why not any others in the past five years?"

"We met just after Christmas. You looked so young and nervous, but you were fierce. You proved yourself to me within thirty seconds."

I smile in the darkness. "You hired me on the spot. Dragged me into your next meeting."

"You made yourself indispensable. I couldn't let you go after that."

"On my first work anniversary, you took me to lunch at Rockefeller. Gave me the watch." I touch my wrist, which feels naked without the Rolex.

"I wanted to give you more." He nuzzles my ear. "I had learned your mom passed away just before we met. That the holiday was important to you."

"But you didn't let me have the holiday this year. Even though you were doing the work with Sandra. I thought you were becoming a kinder, gentler Dread Lord and then… you trapped me here."

He presses his face to my hair. "I'm the worst," he says. He adds something else, but his voice is muffled.

"What?"

"I said, because of Rinaldo."

"Rinaldo?" It takes me a moment to place the name. "Captain of the Thrusters?"

"He asked you out to the New Year's party."

"How did you know?"

"I overheard you and Sloan."

I'm confused. Why are we talking about Rinaldo? Then I feel how tense Piers is. "Wait, are you jealous?"

No answer.

"That's why you turned mean on Tuesday and then dragged me up here." It's all making sense.

"I'm an ogre."

"It's okay," I sigh.

"It's not. You deserve so much better than me." His head is bowed against mine, his breath on the back of my neck.

"No one's irredeemable, Piers. Not even you. But you could've just told me you wanted to spend the holidays with me. You could've just said, "Dammit, Wellesley, my feelings will not be repressed. I want you. I've tried to resist but can no longer." My Mr. Darcy accent isn't working, so I switch to Eliza Doolittle. "Can you Adam and Eve it? Trouble and strife, guv'nor." I add some Cockney rhyming slang for good measure.

"I could not say that, actually. Because that is gibberish."

"Well, you could've said *something*."

"I couldn't, though."

"Why not?"

His sigh shakes my whole body. "Because I'm the worst. I kept imagining you alone, missing your mom, and I couldn't bear it. But that's not all. I thought that on New Year's, you were going to be with him. I thought this was my chance. My last chance to win you."

He wants to win me?

He grips me hard, rubbing my belly, nestling me deeper in his arms like he's afraid I'll turn to mist and slip away. "And I fucked it up. I was selfish." His voice is raw with regret. "I'm sorry. I know it's not enough to apologize for the past five years, but I do regret my behavior."

A genuine apology? From the Dread Lord? I can't breathe.

"I wish I were a better man. For you. But I'm not. I am the Dread Lord."

"The Dread Lord isn't that bad."

"Oh, but he is. He was raised to be cruel and cut down anyone weaker than him. But then he hired this amazing woman to be his assistant. She's brilliant and beautiful, the only person who can make him laugh. She gets him. And she works hard, harder than anyone else, and soon she's the only thing he looks forward to when he wakes each day." His arms tighten around me, not letting me get away. I'm glad he can't see my face because my mouth is hanging open.

"But he's an ogre and doesn't know how to talk about his feelings. He doesn't understand what feelings are. His father told him therapy was for the weak.

"So he drowns himself in work and more work, making money until his pile is bigger than anyone else's. But it doesn't make him happy, nothing does. Except for her. But he doesn't know how to talk to her, so he bullies her mercilessly.

"He wishes he could let her go, but he can't. He's not good enough. But he hates himself for what he puts her through. And every time he sees her, he wants to take care of her.

Because I do, Wellesley. I want to take care of you. I want to give you everything."

"I didn't know."

"I didn't know myself. But I'm trying to be better, Wellesley, for you. That's what Marty said, practically in his last breath. 'Hang on to her. Don't let her go.'"

"Oh." My heartbeat booms in my ears.

"He told me to marry you. Do whatever it takes, he said. Don't let her get away."

My mind goes blank. Me and Piers, married? It does not compute.

"I've cared for you. I've always cared for you, I just didn't know it."

I frown, wanting to shrink back. This isn't making sense. I can't believe he actually wanted to be… with me. "You really want me. You want to be with me."

"Yes. Is that so hard to believe?"

"Honestly? Yes." I can't imagine us together. I mean, I can because I fantasize about it all the time. But in reality? He's a billionaire, and I'm his assistant. Sure, Marty always said it was like I could read Pier's mind. Sloan thinks I'm the only one who can put up with him. But being together is different. "I already told you I'm not cut out to be a trophy wife."

"You wouldn't be a trophy." He squeezes my arms. "You'd be mine."

"I fantasize about you, all the time," I blurt. "All sorts of fantasies. But I never thought—" I pry his hands open so I can turn and face him. "I never thought you felt anything for me."

"Darling." He captures my hand, brings it to his mouth. Kisses it.

I touch his face. He feels real. But I don't know if this is real. And if it is, where do we go from here?

"Wellesley, please. You make me better. I want to be

better. I'll call into town and make sure you're back in the city by tomorrow. Just please tell me I haven't fucked this up. Please tell me I haven't lost you."

I rest my cheek against his chest. I can't speak, but I can let him hold me. It's not an answer, but it's enough for now.

For tomorrow, though? I need a Christmas miracle.

Dear Santa...

I gaze out at the tree and make my wish.

Once again, daylight punches me in the face. The blinds are open, the sun is high, and the glare on the snow is fierce.

It's Christmas morning. I fell asleep in Pier's arms after all those candlelit confessions. My abs and pussy are a bit sore from our amazing sexy times, but other than that, I feel amazing.

Fast asleep, Piers's face looks kinder, more open. I forgive him for his past transgressions, I really do.

But I don't know if we can be together.

What would that even look like?

I don't need to decide right now. Outside the window, the world is sparkling like diamonds. The winter wonderland is calling me. I dress warmly in my HoudZou, thick leggings, and my red boots. And my Santa hat, of course.

Outside, the freezing air wakes me right up. The air is clean and fresh but cold enough to turn my nose into an icicle. I trudge through the thick drifts to the end of the deck and lean on the railing by the Christmas tree. Without the lights on, it looks like a regular tree, but it's still beautiful.

And Piers didn't seem to hate it last night. We made a new memory.

I've cared for you. I've always cared for you, I just didn't know it.

I wish I could call my mom, get her advice. She was always unlucky in love, but she did tell me to find someone who made me laugh, someone who would do anything for me. 'Don't settle,' she said.

Piers does make me laugh, even when he's roasting me. And he certainly went out of his way to trap me here.

The real thing I can't wrap my head around is why he wants me. He's brilliant, sexy, Hollywood handsome. What do I have to offer him?

You're the only one who can take me.

But I'm just his assistant.

Don't do that. Don't put yourself down before anyone else can.

Maybe I need therapy.

I'm pondering this when the sound of jingling bells fills the air. I think I'm imagining it when I glimpse something brown and red moving through the fir trees.

What the...?

I walk down the stairs to get a closer look and end up knee deep in the snow right as four huge brown deer trot into view. They're pulling a bright red sleigh, and the jingling sound is from the bells on their harnesses and antlers.

"Whoa, there," a gruff voice calls, and the sleigh slides to a stop. The sleigh driver is a big and brawny white man wearing a thick burgundy coat edged with white fur. His head is covered by a huge brown fur hat, the sort an old-timey trapper would wear. It matches his big, bristling beard, which is brown with a few white patches.

He pulls out a piece of paper and frowns at it, then looks up at the house while rubbing his beard with a gloved hand.

"Hello?" I call.

His face splits into a grin. "Hello there." His voice booms out. "Merry Christmas. Are you Wellesley Creech?"

I nearly fall over. "Um, yes? That's me."

He stuffs the paper back in his pocket. "Just who I was looking for. I heard you need a ride to the airport. Whoa, Ruddy." This last part he says to one of the big deer, who snorted at me and pawed the snow. "Hang on," Beard Man says. He jumps down and pulls a big burlap sack out of the back of his sleigh. He reaches in and pulls out a fat carrot. "Rudy's a good sort, but she gets antsy if I don't give her snacks."

Rudy? My mouth falls open, but I close it quickly before my tongue freezes. "Are these reindeer?"

"They sure are." He tromps around in his big black boots, feeding each of them a carrot. "Snows a bit deep for a sleigh ride, but they wanted out of the barn."

"So you came to pick me up?" I still can't believe it. Piers mentioned something about figuring out a way to get me back to the city for Christmas, but I told him to just go to bed.

"Heard your boss had you up here, making you work through Christmas. Can't have that." He frowns.

"Um, no, it's okay. He… meant well." *I kept imagining you alone, missing your mom, and I couldn't bear it.*

Rudy shakes her head, making the bells on her antlers jingle. She's not convinced.

Beard Man puts a hand on Rudy's neck to calm her. "So are you ready? If you grab your things, I can have you at the helipad by noon."

This is what I wanted, right? A trip back to NYC. To my cold little apartment and moldy leftovers. No Piers. Just the ache of missing my mom.

Is that what I really want?

Or... do I want to stay in a mansion with a man who professes to be crazy about me?

What do I really want for Christmas? What would I choose if I allowed myself to go after what I want?

I'd choose Piers. But I have to believe I deserve to be with him. That would be a real Christmas miracle. But you know what? 'Tis the season.

Beard Man is waiting for an answer. Even the reindeer look curious. Except Rudy. She looks bored.

"Actually... I'm sorry you came all this way, but I don't need to leave. I'm going to stay."

He raises a bristly brow. "You want to spend Christmas with your boss?"

"He's not my boss anymore, actually. I quit. And... I kind of like it here. With him."

A grin splits the Beard man's face. "All right then, Wellesley. If you change your mind, just call down to the town. Ask for Nick." With a wink, he leaps back in his sleigh, jiggles the reins, and gets the reindeer moving again. Within a few seconds, they disappear down the hill.

My mouth is hanging open again.

Did that just happen? And is that a faint "On Dasher, on Dancer?" I hear with the faint sound of jingling bells?

Maybe I'm still drunk.

"Wellesley?" Piers shouts from the deck above. His voice sounds hoarse.

"I'm here. Down here."

"Thank Christ." He sticks his head over the deck. His hair is mussed, his face taut. He's twisting something between his fingers. "I woke up and couldn't find you. I thought... I thought you'd gone."

"I thought about it." I glance back the way Beard Man went with his reindeer. "I think I just met Santa."

"Have you been drinking again?"

I laugh, a big, bright laugh that bounces off the mountains.

He comes to the top of the stairs, and I realize what he's holding. It's the second Santa hat. "Darling, it's freezing. You're not dressed for this weather."

"I have my HoudZou," I say, spreading my arms. My face is cold, but the rest of me is toasty warm. The hoodie-mumu is amazing; I should really buy stock in the company. "And you have a hat."

"You need to come up here and get back inside."

"You're not the boss of me," I sing-song.

"Wellesley," his voice sharpens.

"Put on the hat, Piers."

"What?"

"Please? For me?"

He shakes it out with a frown but puts it on. He looks good, in his own scary-sexy Dread Lord sort of way. "There. Are you happy?"

"Esctatic."

"Is that all you want?" He glowers down at me from the top step.

"Not even close. Why did you buy the Thrusters?"

His face goes blank.

"My mother's favorite football team, and you bought them, even though they haven't won a championship in ten years. You made sure I could watch every game if I wanted, and from the owner's box. From anyone else, it would be a generous gift, but you pretended it was an investment. And then there was the unlimited clothing budget. And all the meals—dining out or from your private chef."

I've cared for you. I've always cared for you, I just didn't know it.

"You also offered me new housing. I didn't take it—"

"You complained about your apartment all the time, but you didn't want to let it go because that's where you lived with your mom and leaving it would feel like losing her all over again."

I marvel that he figured that out. I didn't realize that about myself until now. "So you made me work late nights because you couldn't bear the idea of me being home alone. Right?"

He swallows and nods. It's one thing to confess all this in the moonlight but another to shout it from a mountainside.

"I think you were taking care of me this whole time. In your own emotionally closed-off way." I wag my finger at him.

He has that lost expression on his face again. "It hasn't all been noble." His gaze falls to his brogues. "I also didn't want to be alone. I wanted to be with you, Wellesley, and if that meant forcing you to stay by my side, dragging you to every godforsaken work event I could…"

"Trapping me in a mansion with you, making sure I couldn't run…"

"I'm sorry—"

"It's okay. I know why you did it." This is the man who found out my mother always took me to Rockefeller Center and made sure to take me there for our work anniversary to make new memories. "By the way, I want my watch back."

His head comes up, his golden eyes alight with hope. "Does that mean… are you—"

"Oh no, I still quit. I'm never ever working for you again. At least, not under you."

His eyes narrow.

"Not in the business sort of way." My face heats. "I would be willing to be under you again, in other ways. I'm ready to make a deal."

"Are you now?"

"Yes. If the terms are good. I learned to negotiate from the best." *Attagirl,* I can hear Marty say.

"Then tell me, Wellesley." He starts slowly walking down the stairs. "What will it take for you to make that deal? Or at least stop this madness and come inside?" The way he's looking at me promises retribution of the sexy kind. My butthole tingles.

"Hmmm," I let my fingers dance against my lips, pondering my demands.

"I'll sell my company," he says before I can think of anything. "Everything. All of Lords. You don't have to quit. I'll make you CEO."

"What?"

"I'll sell it to you right now for a dollar."

"You'd give away all your money for me?"

"Not all my money. I'd still have the trust. The family holdings in London and Mumbai. The ancestral pile," he shudders.

"But everything you've built, you'd give to me?" He worked so hard to make his own pile. To prove himself to his father.

"You're worth it."

Oh, Piers. "I don't want your company."

"Then what do you want?"

You. I could say it. I could shout it. But I don't want to make it too easy for him.

"Come down here," I say. "There's something I want to show you."

I start to back up into the fir trees.

"Wellesley," his voice sharpens. "Get back here."

I turn and run into the woods as fast as the deep snow and my boots will allow.

It doesn't take long for Piers to follow me. "This is ridiculous. If you think you're going to—"

I sock him with a snowball. It hits his perfect cheek and fills his open mouth. He sputters and recovers quickly, but I have plenty of ammunition at hand. I hit him again and again, laughing like a maniac. Finally, he gives up trying to dodge the snowballs and rushes me, and I run shrieking.

He chases me around the forty-foot fir tree. I'm laughing too hard to move fast, but I zigzag and avoid him until my boots betray me. He tackles me, and we both go down. Somehow, he cushions my fall, so I end up on top of him. Snow crusts his brows and wool coat, and his Santa hat is askew. He's never looked more amazing.

I'm about to tell him that when he reaches up and grabs a fir tree branch, showering us with snow.

"You asshole," I sputter. My face is already numb, but I know the snow is cold.

"I am an asshole," he says. "One might even say an ogre. But you can take it."

"You're my ogre," I agree, and let him draw my head down to his for a kiss. By the time we're done, his dick is poking into me through all my layers, and I'm warm enough to pull off my HoudZou and roll in the snow.

"Do you forgive me, darling?"

"I do. For everything. Because… I love you."

He looks stunned.

"You don't have to say it back," I say quickly. "I figure you'll need some more remedial lessons from Sandra before you figure out all your feelings."

"I do, but not for this. I love you, Wellesley. I didn't know it. I just knew I didn't deserve you. I still don't deserve you, but I can't stand the idea of you being with anyone else."

"I don't want to be with anyone else." I lick my lips, feeling happy but scared, a rush of giddy fear like I get when

I stand in a top-floor penthouse looking down over Manhattan. "It's you, Piers. It's always been you."

"It's a goddamn Christmas miracle." He kisses the shit out of me until I'm shivering but not from the cold.

"You want me," I say happily.

"I do. I want you for Christmas. But not just for Christmas. I want you every night and every morning. I want you grouchy, and I want you sweet. I want you in the hot tub and the shower. And in bed. And in front of the fireplace."

"Let's do it. Right now." I roll off him, and he helps me up, tutting at my fashion boots in the snow.

"I'm going to train your replacement," I tell him. "Although it might take more than one person to replace me. Two. Or three."

"You're irreplaceable."

"Yes, I know, that's why I'll still be on your arm for every party and gala. You need me. You need my eyes and ears."

"I need everyone to know you're mine. Be my date to the New Year's party?"

"I will," I laugh. "But I don't know if I'll be ready to leave this house by then."

"Then let's stay. We'll make new memories."

"You have a deal." I seal it with a kiss.

"Now, darling," he says, hoisting me into his arms. "We're going inside. I am going to rip this ridiculous hoodie-mumu off your body and do wicked things to you."

"No, not the Hoodzou," I cry.

His eyes twinkle. "What if I promise to replace it?"

"It's irreplaceable."

"They're made in a factory outside of Shenzhen. I've already bought it."

I gasp. "I was just thinking of investing in them!"

"Let's do it together, then. We'll form a partnership."

"I could model them on my travel blog. Just not in Addis

Ababa. Speaking of which, what if you take some time off work and travel with me?"

"How much time?"

I grin at him, and he sighs. "You drive a hard bargain, my love. But very well."

"We have a deal?"

"Shut up and kiss me."

"You're not the boss of me." But I do.

* * *

DEAR SANTA (or should I call you, Nick?),

THANK YOU. <3

SIGNED,
  The Future Ms. Dread Lord

P.S. You and Rudy and all the reindeer are invited to the wedding. ;)

The End

* * *

AUTHOR'S NOTE:

AHHHHH! Thanks for reading Wellesley & Pier's story! I have had it in my head for some time, and loved how it turned out. I think Beard Man needs a story next, don't you?

Next up in the anthology is Snowed in With the Lumberjack. It's less silly and more cozy and sweet, with my signature spicy scenes, of course.

If you're in the mood for another hot mess heroine and smoldering hero, check out *Her Marine Daddy*, available free at https://www.leesavino.com/lee-savino-freebies.

<3 Lee

SNOWED IN WITH THE LUMBERJACK

I shouldn't be driving in a blizzard. I definitely shouldn't be driving up Snow Mountain.

Now my car's stuck in a ditch, and the only one who can help me is Joel Alder, the reclusive lumberjack who lives in an old hunting cabin deep in the woods.

Joel is three years older than me, and an ex-con. Folk around these parts avoid him, but he's always been kind to me. His strong hands, wild beard, and sun-streaked hair inspire all my dirty fantasies.

Now we're snowed in together. On Christmas Eve. And if I'm a good girl, Joel might make all my naughty dreams come true...

CHAPTER 1

 *ainey*

FAT SNOWFLAKES FLY at my car, too fast for my windshield wipers to clear away. To my right, hemlocks bow under the weight of several blizzards' worth of the white stuff. The dark forest and snowy drifts create a winter wonderland, as picturesque as a Christmas card.

My car's chosen a beautiful place to skid off the road.

I press the gas pedal and the engine whirs. My tires spin. I've just made my predicament worse.

One more attempt, and I turn off the car. The windshield wipers switch off and snow sticks to the glass. The cold seeps in, too. Pretty soon the interior of my car will be below freezing.

I fight to open my door. My car is canted towards the passenger side, half in the ditch. I swing my legs around and land in shin-deep snow. The fluffy flakes aren't so pretty when they're coating my jeans and falling into the tops of my

Ugg boots. I clamber out of my Kia, grabbing my purse as I go.

My little car makes a sad sight, stuck in the ditch. Soon it'll be a white lump and no one will be the wiser. Snow covers everything and makes it beautiful, hiding the sorry state of affairs underneath. My accident will be hidden until things thaw.

I followed truck tracks to get this far up the mountain, but a new layer of snow is obliterating them. This road doesn't get plowed much, if ever. If you ask folks in town who lives up here, they'd say, "No one."

They'd be wrong. Up somewhere on this side of the mountain is an old hunter's cabin. That's where I'll find warmth, and help. That's where I'll find someone who can make a call for me. My cell doesn't get service in this remote part of town.

The wind picks up and drives the snow faster into my face. The flakes stick to my eyelashes and I blink, fighting to keep my eyesight clear. I duck between the hemlocks, gripping my parka tighter around me and wishing I had brought gloves.

Maybe this wasn't such a good idea. I didn't even make it halfway up the mountain, and it's colder out here than I expected. My winter coat might as well be a bikini for all it's doing to keep me warm.

I trudge through the shadowy woods. A hundred steps in, and I have a hitch in my side. I read somewhere that tracking through snow on cross-country skis burns more calories than any other activity, and I don't even have the skis. My body heats up fast, making my skin itch with exertion and sweat. My boots are clogged with snow and my thighs ache with the extra weight.

The forest is silent, all life buried under the white shroud. The only sounds are the huffs and hitches of my breathing and, under my coat, my thumping heart. I follow what looks like a path through the pines. With any luck, it'll bring me to safety. If not...

The last of the light is disappearing through the trees when the trail turns and reveals a dark wooden hut. Its sides are mounted up with snow, and the windows are dark too, but a thin wisp of smoke trickles from the chimney.

A thwacking sound breaks the quiet. For a second I think I've imagined it, but it comes again, a hollow thud. The sound of an ax hitting wood.

"Hello?" I shiver in my boots, resisting the urge to dance back and forth. I can't feel my toes.

A shadow slants between the black tree trunks. In the low light, he looks like a frost giant with an ax in hand and snowflakes clinging to his beard. Joel Adler, the man I hoped to see.

The man of my dreams.

"Lainey," he asks in a deep voice, "what are you doing here?"

oel

"MY CAR BROKE DOWN," she says. It's Lainey Stevens from town, shivering in a snow drift, with flakes crusting her clothes. Her teeth clack together.

I swear before I can stop myself, and sink my ax into a log. I stalk forward, watching her closely, but she never flinches. Other people in town give me a wide berth, but not Lainey. She works the register at her aunt Gemma's grocery store. I see her every time I drive down to buy supplies.

"Jesus, it's freezing out here." My voice sounds harsh, unused. Not many people to talk to up here. Not many people want to talk to me when I'm in town. Only Gemma Stevens… and Lainey. "Where are your gloves?"

She stares up at me, her wide eyes fringed with black lashes. Her lips are tinged with blue.

I jerk my head towards my cabin. "Get inside."

She stumbles and I reach for her, stopping myself at the last moment. No reason to put my hands on her.

"Sorry," she squeaks, and my soul wilts a little. She's intimidated by me, even though I've been as gentle and considerate as I can be. But of course she is. Everyone knows I'm an ex-con. A felon.

And now she's on my mountain, fifteen feet from my home. Alone. Any woman would be nervous.

"I'm not going to hurt you," I growl. I sound like a psycho.

"I know." She stops and stares up at me, and a line appears between her brows. Is she glaring at me? "You would never hurt me, Joel Adler."

She's scolding me.

"All right." I can't stop my smile, and I'm glad it's hidden behind my beard. I've never been berated by someone a foot smaller and a hundred pounds lighter than me. "As long as we're clear."

I take her hand. If she's not afraid of me, she won't mind a gentle touch.

Her fingers are little icicles in mine. I suck in a breath.

"Sorry," she says again.

"Don't apologize." I propel her forward, practically hauling her off her feet in my haste to bustle her inside. When she staggers again, I scoop her up into my arms and carry her across the cabin threshold like a groom with his fairytale bride.

I kick the heavy door hard so it swings open without sticking. Snow spills off the roof, narrowly missing us. I duck inside and carry my precious bundle straight to my butt-ugly orange couch in front of the fireplace.

"Stay here," I order, and rise to shut the door and knock snow off my boots. I return and tug hers off, tossing them to dry by the fire. I'll mop up the piles of melting snow later.

I help her out of her coat and hang it up close to the hearth. "What were you thinking, hiking up here?"

"I couldn't get cell service on the road."

I bite back another curse. I need to watch my foul mouth. "Why were you even driving in this?"

"It wasn't so bad in town." Her gaze is fixed on the floorboards at her socked feet. She's like that when I visit her aunt's shop, peeking out from behind the books she reads in between dealing with customers. She's shy, and looks young for her age. I'd think she was in her teens if I didn't know she was only a few years behind me in high school. We were in a junior English class together, because she was advanced and I was a senior with straight Ds in every class, barely scraping by. That was Lainey—smarter than the whole school, and better than me by a mile.

Ten years, and not much has changed.

"Let's get you warm." I can't think when she's shivering. I pull an old quilt off the couch and wrap it around her, then crouch to rub her hands.

"I'm okay," she whispers.

"You could've fucking died," I growl.

She has nothing to say to that. We sit in silence, her on the ugliest couch ever made, me on the floor.

My hands are battered and scarred, marred with the blue tattoo ink I got in prison. More of my bad decisions, written on my skin.

Her fingers are perfect—small, and tipped with glossy nails filed to neat crescents.

I can't stand the contrast between her hands and mine, so I leave her side to throw more logs on the fire. When I turn back to her, she's pulled off her snow-dusted hat, releasing a waterfall of silky dark hair. Her cheeks are pink under the black crescents of her eyelashes. In the firelight, Lainey glows like a jewel.

My breath saws in my chest. Next to her angelic perfection, my home is worn and dingy, one step away from decrepit. I spent the last year renovating it, fixing sections of rotten wood. My grandfather used it as a hunting cabin. There's no mention of the structure on the land deed he willed to me—either he'd forgotten it, or thought it had rotted away. I furnished the place with castoffs I found at the dump. I knew it was no palace, but I see it now through Lainey's eyes, and I'm ashamed.

No one's been up here for years, no one but me. The closest anyone's come was Lainey, six months ago, in summer.

Shame makes me snap. "You shouldn't have been on the road tonight."

"I was going to see Aunt Gemma," she stammers. "It's Christmas."

"You're from here. You know what the storms are like," I chastise her.

She bites her lip and looks to the window. The glass panes are choked with white, but there's a small dark center that shows white flakes flurrying through the night.

I want to do a lot more than scold her so I force myself to head for the door.

"I'm getting more wood," I say without turning. "Stay by the fire. It's snowing like crazy, and there's no way a truck can get up here before they plow the road. Looks like you're here for the night."

* * *

Lainey

. . .

TEN MINUTES in Joel's house and I've already screwed up. He scowls as he tells me to stay, as if the thought of sharing his home with me for the night disgusts him. The door slams behind him.

I palm my cheeks. Am I so repulsive? Such awful company?

My hair is tangled and the ends are wet from melting snow. I push the mass back and adjust the old quilt he threw over me. I'm wearing my nicest sweater and favorite pair of jeans. The fuzzy wool and denim are buttery soft and fall nicely over my curves, highlighting the swell of my breasts and butt, hiding the rest.

In high school, Joel was a chick magnet. He didn't have to chase girls, they flocked to him. Blondes or brunettes, pink-haired emo goth wannabes or the most prissy cheerleaders—he didn't seem to have a preference. He didn't care if you had a boyfriend or were flirting with him to make your crush jealous. He'd be down for a quickie in his old Corvette, the one he bought at auction and pieced back together with parts he scavenged from the junkyard. It had different colored doors but was still an awesome ride.

No one was surprised when he got busted for jacking cars. What was more surprising was that after he did his time for grand larceny, he came back to our little town.

"Where else would he go?" my aunt Gemma snorted when a customer gossiped about this in front of her. "He always liked the woods."

I'd always had a crush on Joel Adler, the coolest boy in school. But that was the first time I saw him for more than his facade, the sexy charm boy who was always down for a fuck or a fight. I remembered how he created works of art in shop class: birdhouses and stools and even a cradle, made with honey-stained wood.

The next time he came into Aunt Gemma's store, I summoned my courage and gave him a smile.

The cabin door swings open, letting in a blast of frozen air. I summon my habitual smile but it falters in the frozen stare of my host. He comes in, blowing smoke and glowering at me like a frost giant who's found an intruder in his lair.

His cold stare doesn't cool his hotness one degree. If Joel was gorgeous as a boy, he's breathtaking as a man. Tall, with lean muscles, and thick brown hair striated with red and blond like rare wood. Eyes a striking, crystalline blue.

He stomps past, carrying a stack of wood that looks like it weighs more than I do. The only sounds are the crackle of the flame-eaten logs, and his harsh breathing.

I knot my fingers together. I've messed up and I don't know how to make it right. So I sit in silence and watch Joel stack wood. Once he's done, he strips off his coat and toes off his boots, and my own breaths grow heavy. He's got a flannel shirt on, and while I watch, he loosens the button and rolls up his sleeves. He's not bulky, but he's strong. Sleek as a mountain lion. Even the indigo smudges of his prison tattoos lurking under the crisp, gold-tinted hairs on his powerful forearms are sexy. Another layer to the enigma that is Joel Adler.

I've always liked puzzles. Mystery novels, or romances with anti-heroes. Chapters with layer upon layer of intrigue my intellect can sink into. The blessing and curse of the voracious bookworm: a life lived sitting in corners, hiding between the pages, reading instead of living life.

One more semester, and I'll graduate with my Masters in Library Science. I'll move out of my parents' summer home, find a job, wear frumpy sweaters and pencil skirts, adopt a succulent and a cat. Become a cliche.

The only blip on my horizon, the only piece that doesn't fit, is Joel Adler. Another woman would know exactly what to say to him. She'd be cuddled right up with him on the couch.

"Are you cold?" he asks, staring at the fire as if it'll give him the answers.

"I'm good." My voice is soft.

Coming here was a mistake. I know that now. Some adventures are best left to heroines in books.

I shift on the couch, and a paperback flops from the quilt's folds to the floor. The cover's torn off, but I recognize the font.

I slide off the couch to my knees to rescue the book, a familiar friend. *"Secrets of a Summer Night."* I pick it up and smooth the pages. "I love Lisa Kleypas. Were you reading this?"

From my position kneeling on the floor, Joel looms even taller. His blue eyes burn and his nostrils flare.

"Get up." He motions me back to the couch.

I catch my apology before it escapes and obey, but he's already moved away to another part of the cabin. This place is one open room. He can't escape me, not unless he goes back out to chop wood. And he's already used that excuse.

He stands in the kitchen area of the cabin, as far away from me as he can get without heading into the cold. I've made him upset. How? Why?

I clutch the book to my heart. Books are easy. Books, I understand. "I love this book. I reread it all the time."

"I know," he says, his back still to me. "I've seen you read it. You gave me that copy, remember?"

"Oh..." I do remember. I keep a stack of paperbacks by the register to read and reread. Sometimes I give them to customers. Why didn't I remember I gave this to Joel?

I'm so flustered, I open the book and read a few lines. I don't look up until Joel's shadow falls over me.

His voice echoes in my ears and I realize he's been calling my name.

"Sorry—"

"No apologizing," he corrects me gently, and plucks the paperback from my hands. I would protest and clutch it to my chest like a safety blanket, but he replaces it with my second favorite thing in the world: a mug of tea.

So that's what he was doing in the kitchen corner of the cabin. Making me tea. Loose-leaf Earl Grey, from the smell of it, in a carefully knotted teabag. I bury my face in the fragrant steam.

Joel remains standing, cradling the book in his palms. His fingers are long and elegant, even rough with scars and tattoos. A craftsman's hands. "And yes. To answer your question. I was reading this."

"Really? I mean…" I stammer. "I didn't mean to imply I didn't think you'd read it."

"It's okay. I didn't used to read like I do now. Picked it up in prison." He glances at me then, checking for a reaction. Does he expect me to shy away from the reminder he did time?

"If you like that book, you'd like the whole series. I have a whole list of favorites."

"A whole list?" There's a hint of a smile under his beard. He's teasing me.

"She's good," I defend. "Everyone loves *A Devil in Winter*. But my favorite is *Marrying Winterborne*."

"I'll check it out. Drink your tea."

I sip the hot liquid. It occurs to me that he keeps issuing orders and I obey without thinking. "This tea is really good." The kitchen takes up one corner of the cabin, to the right of the door. The fireplace and couch are opposite. In the middle of the room is a wooden table with a single chair. Beyond that, in the far right corner, is a big bed.

I snap my gaze back to the fire and meet Joel's ice-blue eyes. My cheeks burn, knowing he watched me snoop.

Awkward girl is awkward. Why did I think tonight would be any different? It would take a lot of Christmas magic to fix my dorkiness.

"I've never been here before," I mumble to my tea.

"No one has." Joel sets the paperback on the mantle. "Kinda the point of living alone on a mountain. The privacy."

I set my mug on the floor, feeling ill. "You're angry with me. I shouldn't have come."

"No, Lainey." He crouches in front of me and closes his hands around mine. "I'm an asshole."

oel

LAINEY LOOKS SO MISERABLE, I'm ready to banish myself from my own home. Instead, I warm her fingers between mine. She's not as frozen, and a lot of my tension eases out of me knowing she's warming up.

"You scared me," I admit.

"What?"

"It's dangerous for you to be out on the road, in the snow. You could've died. Why aren't you with your family?"

"My parents are in Arizona."

"Right." I knew that. It's wrong, how much I eavesdrop on Gemma and Lainey's conversations. How much I keep tabs on Lainey. "They own a place there now."

"Yes."

Acid fills my mouth but I make myself ask the next question, "Why aren't you with your boyfriend?"

"With Landon?"

Landon. A frat boy with no chin who thinks he's hot shit because his dad owns some strip malls a few towns over and dips his toes into politics. When Landon visits Lainey at the store, he parks his red Mercedes in the Reserved for the Disabled spot.

"We broke up."

"You dumped him?" I settle beside her on the couch.

"I... It was mutual." Her gaze drops away, her shyness tinged with shame. "He wanted more than I wanted to give."

Heat flares in my chest. "Did he do something to you?"

"I'm okay, Joel," she says quickly, as if she recognizes there's a monster inside me roaring to be let out. "He didn't do anything."

I make a note to check if she's telling the whole truth, or downplaying it to be nice. If Landon hurt her, I'll kill him with my bare hands.

It'd be so easy. Hang around one of the ratty college bars on a Friday night and wait for him to stagger out drunk. Hit him over the head or choke him out, and secure him in the trunk of a throwaway car. I live on a ton of private land. It's easy to hide a body in these woods.

"Joel." She puts her hand on mine, and my murderous visions fade away.

"It's fine. It just wasn't working out."

"You're too good for him." Her hand is delicate, pure, in my dirty palm, but I can't let her go.

"It's nice of you to say that."

"It's true. You're too good for anybody in this town."

Her long lashes flutter. She doesn't believe me. I shouldn't touch her but I can't let this pass.

"You're perfect." And she is. Dark hair, dark eyes, pure skin. Lush curves under the bulky sweaters she wears. She zoomed through high school and college, graduating early. She's only working at the grocery store to pay the bills and help out her aunt. Soon she'll have her Masters and be done with our small town.

Lainey Stevens is going places. Me? I'm an ex-con, living like a hermit on a deserted mountain. I might as well be a million years older than her. I fix up old cars and sell them at a profit, making enough so I don't have to count coins when I buy ground beef and tomato sauce at Gemma's store. Lainey's so high above me she might as well be in the clouds.

But she doesn't seem to understand that. She shrugs off my compliment.

I grasp her chin, forcing her to look at me. "It's true. Lainey, listen to me." I wait until her gaze meets mine. "You are perfect. You are. Don't let anyone tell you otherwise." Our faces are inches apart, her breath sweet on my lips. "Do you understand? Say *yes, Joel.*"

"Yes, Joel."

Damn, if that doesn't get me hard.

Her tongue darts out and licks her top lip, glazing it. She has a perfect mouth with thick and curvy lips. I bet her pussy looks the same.

I'm so busy fantasizing about her pussy, I almost miss her little laugh.

"You're always lecturing me. Remember the last time my car broke down?"

I do, vividly. The summer heat, and her bent over to check her tires, her dress hitching up the back of her curvy calves and delicious rear. She wore a white cardigan and looked modest and sexy at the same time. "You were driving up here with bald tires. You deserved a lot more than a lecture."

She's looking at the floor again, instead of at me. "You said if it happened again… I'd be in trouble."

"I said more than that. I told you if you ever drove on bald tires again, I'd turn you over my knee." I wait for her to run, screaming. Instead, her breath hitches and her lips curve.

I save us both from the silence. "I'll take a look at your car before they tow it. I might be able to fix it. Your car and I have a good relationship."

"You're always rescuing me."

I rise, because I can't sit close to her any longer. My dick makes it too uncomfortable. "Right. You're going to sit cozy. I'm going to feed you. And in the morning, I'll trek out to call for a tow. If the roads are good, I'll take you home. I can try to text Gemma now, so she's not worried."

"Okay." She sounds reluctant. "I texted her too. She won't be worried."

Something about her tone strikes me as off, but I don't think too hard about it. After I've fired off the text, I serve her a bowl of beef stew and hover over her to make sure she eats. "You're lucky I was here tonight," I say, picking at my own stew. I don't want to think about what would have happened if she'd been stuck up here alone.

"I heard you tell Gemma you'd be home for Christmas," she blurts, and ducks her head.

I rock back on my heels, feeling amused that she eavesdropped on me, just like I do with her. I might go grocery shopping more than I need to, just to see her.

I take her bowl and hand her back the book to read while I wash up. I'm mopping up the wet spots where the snow melted on the floor when what Lainey said earlier lands.

I might not be book smart like Lainey, but I have my own brand of smarts. Lainey's good at a lot of things, but lying isn't one of them.

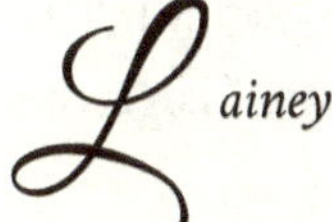

ainey

JOEL LOOMS OVER ME. "You lied to me, Lainey." He looks so stern. "Gemma isn't in town for the holidays. She flew out to be with your parents."

I swallow. I've spent the last few minutes trying to think up excuses and pretending to read.

He takes the book out of my hand and sets it aside. "What's really going on here?"

"You said you'd be alone." I knot my fingers together. "It's Christmas."

His brows slant down.

"No one should be alone on Christmas." I resist the urge to squirm under his fierce stare. *Be bold.* "So I came up here."

"You came up here," he repeats slowly.

"I want to be with you." And I put my hand on his leg. A tremor runs through me. Or maybe him. Or both of us.

"Fuck," he breathes. "You did this on purpose."

"I didn't mean to break down. I was hoping to find the road."

"You could have been hit by a car. Or gotten lost in the woods." The tops of his cheeks flare red. He lets out a gust of air and motions sharply. "Stand up."

I rise and he takes my place, immediately grabbing my hand to guide me down into his lap.

His l*ap.*

"Wh-what—"

"It seems my first lecture didn't take hold. So I'm going to give it again… with a little reinforcement."

"Reinforcement?"

"Oh, yes." His hand skates up my back. "It's time you learned your lesson. I promised you punishment, didn't I?" When I don't answer, he gives me a squeeze. "Isn't that right?"

I nod.

"Use your words, babygirl."

My face has to be bright red. I squeeze my thighs together. "Yes. That's right." I'm breathless and my heart's galloping. I'm on Joel Adler's lap, staring into stern blue eyes inches from mine. I have no idea what's going to happen, but there's no place I'd rather be. "You said you'd turn me over your knee."

His grip tightens but his face is calm. "Good girl. Tell me, Lainey. Have you ever been spanked?"

I shake my head before I remember to answer. "No."

"In a minute, I'm going to help you up. I'm going to unbutton your jeans, but I won't undress you yet. You're going to lie across my lap. I'll spank you over this," he rubs the denim stretched over my hip, "first. Warm you up. Then, you'll get punished."

"Will it hurt?" I squeak. I'm six seconds away from hyperventilating.

"Oh, yes." His breath ghosts across my ear. "That's why it's a punishment. "But if you take it like a good girl…" he leans back and tucks a thick strand of hair behind my ear, "I'll give you a reward."

Did I know this was going to happen when I drove up the mountain? Some part of me knew that even if I made the first move, Joel would take me on his terms. But I never imagined this, not even in my wildest fantasies—most of which starred Joel.

"Are you ready?" He doesn't wait for the answer. He's already guiding me up and doing exactly what he said he'd do.

I can't stand to look at him when he undoes my jeans button and pulls down the zipper. His knuckles brush the soft bulge of my belly and there's a sharp ache right in my core. I need him to go further. But I'm afraid of what will happen when he does.

He eases me over his lap, face down this time, so my stomach rests on the hard and powerful muscles of his legs. He tips me over so I'm a little off balance. I'm two sides of a triangle and my ample rear end is the apex, pointed up right at him. Not a flattering position. I'm used to hiding, using sweatshirts to cover up my softness and size.

His fingers ghost up my thigh, and my skin prickles under the thin layer of denim.

"You're so beautiful," he mutters. Each pass of his hand wakes my body up, bringing it to life. I never knew my bottom had so many nerve endings. "I can't believe this is happening."

Same, Joel. Same.

Something prods my stomach. It's his dick. I shift so I'm not crushing it, but he steadies me with a hand in the small of my back. I'm clutching his leg, off balance, and wait for his hand to descend.

The first few smacks over my jeans are underwhelming. His palm claps down with a thuddy sound. There's sensation but there's no pain.

"Ready for more?"

"Yes."

He chuckles. "I should have known. Let's get these jeans off you."

I start to rise and his hand on my back turns to steel.

"No." He holds me down and yanks off my jeans somehow, scooting them over my hips. Now my face is really red. I'm ass-up and totally exposed. I wore my best underwear—a blush-pink bra and panty set. I didn't anticipate this happening, but I'd hoped *something* would.

"Pink." He sounds like he's been punched in the gut. He trails his fingers across my bottom, exploring. My panties are so thin, I feel everything. The way his rough callouses catch on my soft skin. There's reverence in the way he touches me.

His palm crashes down, and the air goes out of my lungs. He peppers my bottom with sharp, stinging smacks. Tears spring into my eyes.

But a part of me is satisfied. *This is more like it.* He said this was punishment. Punishment shouldn't be fun. This is the way I earn my reward. And I love to strive and earn things. To prove myself.

"This is what happens to naughty girls who disobey me." He spanks in a rhythm, harder when he wants to emphasize something. "You'll remember my lecture this time, Lainey. You'll never put yourself in danger again."

Yes, yes, yes. I can't speak. I can't breathe.

The flat of his hand claps my bottom, hard, sending fire shooting through me. "Your ass is getting nice and pink for me."

My breath rushes out of me in a half gasp. Am I laughing?

Crying? This is so weird. The humiliation and intimacy all rolled into one.

He pulls down my panties and I freeze up again, imaging my big dimpled bottom on display. His hand skates across my skin, barely touching me. I want to wiggle away from him but he catches me before I even try.

"You're almost done with your punishment. And then..." He dips his fingers between my legs, brushing the pouting lips of my pussy. All the air leaves the room. "Breathe, Lainey."

He lets his palm crash down on one cheek and then the other, covering every part of my bottom and even the tops of my thighs. I kick my feet and writhe, but he winds a leg around mine, pinning me so that I'm still. He's way stronger than I am.

The part of me that's fighting gives up and lets go. My thoughts float away, too. There's nothing but Joel's body wrapped around mine, and the punishing kiss of his hand on my skin that sparks heat and pain.

I float in a warm haze. I don't realize he stopped spanking me until he strokes my labia again and a different sensation sings through me. His skilled fingers dance over my intimate parts, finding my clit and painting it with my own wetness. This is so different to when I touch myself, or the few fumbling attempts my ex made. With Logan, if my clit was in Kansas, his finger would be at the North or South Pole.

"You did good for me, taking your punishment." He takes one of my lower lips between his thumb and forefinger, and rubs. "Now it's time for your reward." I'm restless, shifting on his legs again. He clamps his limbs down and holds me so that I can't slide away. Unable to move, I'm forced to focus on the feelings. He tickles my clit and circles it, rubbing at the itchiest spots, making the neediness build in my limbs until a little golden pulse flares through me and satisfaction floods my core. My lips part and my breath comes in a rush. The first pulse is followed by another, and another. And all the while, Joel rubs my back, murmuring, "Good girl."

I'm wobbly when he pulls off my underwear and jeans and eases me back up. My face is flushed from being upside down. My hair is a lost cause.

"Whoa," I breathe, and his eyes crinkle.

He holds my gaze as he licks his fingers. I'm too blissed out to feel embarrassed.

"There's another reason I came up here tonight," I tell him. He's clothed, and I'm naked from my hips down. Not quite my fantasy, but we're a quarter of the way there.

He inclines his head, the flinty spark in his Arctic gaze warning me to tell him the whole truth. My bottom throbs.

"I wanted to give you a gift." I pause but he doesn't guess what I wanted to give him. I'll have to spell it out. Problem is, I don't think I can say it out loud.

I grab the hem of my sweater and pull it over my head. It drops to the floor. I wait, wearing nothing but my blush-pink bra. *Please, please, get what I'm trying to tell you.*

Understanding lights his eyes. He grips my hips and pulls me closer to him. "This is what you want?" There's a rough edge to his voice. Underneath my burning bottom, his dick surges.

"Actually," I say, "it's more like a gift you could give me. Because…" the word sticks in my throat, "I've never done it before."

His eyes flare, then narrow. "Lainey… are you telling me you're a virgin?"

I bob my head up and down, and remember to use my words. "Yes."

"Holy hell." His hands fall away from me, shocking my skin with a sudden rush of cold.

CHAPTER 5

oel

LAINEY SITS ON MY LAP, her bare skin glowing in the firelight. She looks like an angel, an apparition, an emissary from heaven come to bless the faithful. Except I'd be the last person an angel would visit.

And yet here she is, midnight eyes and hair, unwrapped in my lap like a gift.

She came up here to seduce me.

I can't move. I can't speak. I can't think.

After a moment, she shivers and wraps her arms around herself. Her chin drops. "Please don't say no."

I gather her to me immediately, sliding my arms around her. "No. No. I'd never say no to you." She collapses against me and I encourage her to, pulling her chest flush to mine and stroking her hair. "I don't think I'm capable of it."

She shudders, and I feel the emotions filling her to the brim. She's been through a lot in the last hour. I keep her cradled against me for a while, stroking my hand up and down her back. Eventually, I can't resist rubbing her bottom, exploring the marks I left on her, but she doesn't seem to mind. She relaxes further.

I glide my hand over her body, finding my way to the seam between her legs. I shift her in my lap, easing her thighs apart and soothing them until they relax and fall open.

The scent of her arousal rises, and I grit my teeth so I don't come in my pants. I haven't had to fight an orgasm like this since I was a teen, and even then I didn't have to fight this hard. Lainey destroys my control.

"You're going to give me this," I cup my palm over her sweet pussy, "for Christmas?" She's hot and pulsing and oh so wet in my hand. My rough, tattooed hand. The contrast of her perfection against my ugly flesh should make me want to look away. Instead, it gets me hotter. "This most perfect gift... for me?"

She squirms but her lashes lift and she looks squarely at me. "Yes. I want you..." her voice wobbles and she musters more strength, "I want you to have it. To have me."

I wait for her to change her mind. *She's not drunk. She's alone but she drove up here. For me. She hasn't said no. She took off her shirt.*

And as I stare, her chin lifts another inch.

She wants this.

I can't wait a second longer. I scoop her up and stride to my bed, where I lay her out like the virgin offering she is.

As I stare down at her, I know two things: I'm going to hell for this. But it'll be worth it.

She's so soft and sweet—chubby thighs and belly, lush breasts spilling out of the top of her sexy bra, lying on my faded flannel sheets. I can't resist her.

This is a dream. In the morning, she'll be gone.

But right now, she's here. My angel. My miracle on a dark and sacred night.

I lean down and kiss the inside of her knee. She squirms and kicks, unused to being worshiped. If I get my way, she'll get used to it. I'll work my way up her gorgeous body, pleasuring every inch of her. I'll tie her down if I have to. My bed posts are sturdy. And tomorrow—

No. There'll be no tomorrow. This gift, this miracle, is only for one night. I need to make the best of it.

So I get comfy between her legs. When she tries to inch her knees closed, I part her thighs so her pussy blossoms. The scent of her is the sweetest perfume. I kiss a line from her knee to inches from her dripping center, my beard scraping up the sensitive flesh until it's chafed pink. I like my mark on her.

"Joel," she breathes. Her hands come to rest on my head. If she tries to push me away, I'll pin them down, but for now I like how her fingers tangle in my hair, ready to hold on tight. "You don't have to go slow for me. You can—"

"Shhh, babygirl." I stroke two fingers up and down her outer pussy lips, rubbing them with the lightest touch. She's shaved smooth, and ultra sensitive. She torques her hips one way, then the other, and I steady her with a hand at her waist. "There's no rush. This is for me."

"But—"

"No talking." I make it an order, and don't miss how her pussy gushes in response. *Beautiful.* I scoot further to the apex of her thighs. "I'm going to get to know you. Inside and out." I take one labia between a thumb and forefinger and rub until she can't catch a breath. I nuzzle the inside of her knee, nipping her tender flesh. She's spread before me like a book, and I want to read every chapter. Study every paragraph. Memorize every line.

There are faint stretch marks on the curves of her hips

and insides of her thighs. I trace them, first with my fingers, then with my tongue. She makes the most adorable little whimpers and squeals. Is she embarrassed about her body? Her responses? At one point she tries to roll on her front. I spank her sweet ass. "No. No hiding from me."

It takes her a moment to obey. I give her another swat and her rear jiggles so nicely, I spank it some more. The redness from her spanking has faded to a pink flush. It'll be interesting to see how much punishment she can take. She rocks back into position before I can imprint a red mark in the shape of my hand on her bottom.

Her eyes are dark as night, her lips glossy from biting them.

"Relax. I'm going to make this good for you." I slide my palms under her ass, gripping her punished flesh in a reminder of what happens when she disobeys me. I need her to let go, to give me control. Erotic pain can unlock some people better than pleasure can. I suspect it works that way for Lainey.

I let my beard brush over the crease of her thighs, teasing her, circling her wet center. Her scent envelopes me until I'm drunk with it. I thumb her pussy lips until she's restless and desperate, not for escape, but for more.

That's when I lick her. She tenses up but I wear her down, massaging her intimate folds with the lightest touches of my fingertips and tongue. I tickle her clit and taste her from the top of her labia to the bottom. I prop her hips up higher and lick in long, rhythmic strokes. Up and down, up and down, until her hips rock with each pass.

Every so often, she lets out a little coo or sigh. She's been such a good girl, keeping quiet this whole time.

I take a break and lean back, spreading her labia to drink in the view. Her little clit is swollen and needy.

"I want you to come. You can cry out if you want, but the

only thing you say is my name. Got it?" I punctuate my command with a light smack, right on top of her clit.

She gasps.

"Nod if you understand."

She nods so hard, her hair flops into her face.

"Hang on, babygirl." I dive back in, licking her in the same rhythm until she's at a simmer.

"Joel," she hums my name at a volume barely above a whisper. I lick lower, and delve a thumb to massage the shiny skin around the knot of her anal entrance. All of her is mine. Mine to explore. Mine to possess. Mine to fuck.

"Joel!" She clenches her bottom cheeks, trying to squeeze herself shut, but I press my face to her pussy, driving my tongue into her channel to lick up all the juices there. Her hips judder, her whole body vibrating at peak intensity. She turns my name into a moan. I squeeze her ass in rhythm to my tongue fucking her.

She finds my head, digging her fingers into my hair and tugging hard enough to rip it out by the roots. I don't stop. She's panting my name, singing it out as her muscles clench.

"That's it, baby," I say, my mouth filled with her pussy. She jerks, coming undone on my tongue. Her cries are the sweetest music.

I rise up, beard dripping, and crowd closer, making her legs stretch wide. Her pussy is hot and sopping wet in my palm. I've penetrated her with my tongue. She's loose from her orgasms, but she needs more preparation before I give her my dick.

I slip a finger inside, collecting the wetness. I add another and watch her face—the flutter of her eyelashes, the tiny wince in the corner of her mouth.

"You can take me," I tell her, and the wrinkle between her brows disappears. She's so damn responsive to my commands.

We stay like that, joined by my fingers inside her. I toy with her, exploring her wet heat, hooking a finger around to find the rough patch on the front wall of her pussy and swirling over the ridges until it swells.

She's already come twice, her pleasure painted pink on cheeks and chest. The next time she comes, I'll be inside her.

"I'm going to put my dick here," I tell her, being crude on purpose. I have three fingers at her entrance, stretching her. "Inside you. I'm the only man who will have you this way."

Now and forever. The thought flashes through my mind, and I push it away.

She nods, looking nervous and eager at the same time. It's too much. I slide my fingers out of her and yank off my flannel shirt so fast, I lose a few buttons. My undershirt and jeans get tossed on the pile. Her eyes widen at the sight of my dick but she doesn't scramble away.

I fist my cock, squeezing hard to stay my orgasm. This isn't about me. It's about her. I've gotta make this good for her. I can't forget myself.

I get close enough to run a finger over the soft pad of her lips. "One day, I'll fuck you here."

Her eyes grow heavy and her lips part, allowing my finger to penetrate her mouth.

Fuck. If I don't stop now, I'm going to blow.

She reaches for me then hesitates.

"You can touch me, baby. I want you to."

"Like this?" She runs a finger up the side of my dick and it jerks. She pulls away, so I take her hand and guide it. Her fingers are small and dainty, and the sight of them clutching my cock threatens to make me explode.

I cast about for something to distract me. Anything. "The last time you tried to come up here. This summer, when you got a flat. Were you…?"

"Trying to give you my virginity?" She nods. "That was attempt number one."

And I lectured her about her tires and sent her home. "I'm an idiot."

"My seduction technique needs work." She touches her thumb to the head of my dick, gathering the precum and spreading it around. Then she wraps her fingers around the shaft and gives it a tug.

My thighs tremble as I fight the urge to spill in her hand. "Your technique is just fine." I pull her hand away. "You're too good."

She narrows her eyes like she doesn't believe me. I trace her soft lips again.

"Before, when you were on your knees… I couldn't stop thinking of this. Then I hated myself for it," I tell her.

"Why?"

"How can someone like me ever hope to deserve you?"

She grabs my hand and kisses it. "I want you."

I shift so I can line myself up with her pussy. It's now or never, or I'm gonna come on my sheets.

I stop. "I don't have a condom." How could I be so stupid? This cabin has been my haven, my place of hibernation. I live like a monk. "I've never had a girl up here."

"It's okay." Lainey's hips jerk towards mine, silently begging. "I'm on the pill."

"I've been tested. I don't have anything. Any STDs."

"Neither do I," she tells me, solemn.

I pass a hand over her, memorizing the curve of her belly, the generous swell of her hips. My work-rough hands are tanned and stained with ink, obscene beside her pure flesh. An angel and an abomination. The sacred and the profane.

There's no redemption for a man like me. Lainey is as close to heaven as I'll ever come.

But I'm damned if I can't stop myself from possessing her all the way.

CHAPTER 6

JOEL LOOMS OVER ME, his hands on each one of my knees. He sits between my legs like I always imagined. My thoughts are slow and loopy as my body sinks further into the comfortable bed. I want to stay here forever.

"I'll need to go slow," he rasps. "I don't want to hurt you."

"I don't want you to hold back. I want it all." I've risked this much and come so far. We're not stopping now.

I prop myself up and reach for him, draw him down, and kiss me. His beard scrapes my face. I taste myself on his lips, a musky and sharp flavor, with a hint of Joel underneath.

"I want this," I whisper into his mouth, and that seems to be enough.

He shifts himself over me. "All right, Lainey. All right." His hand comes to my left breast, the ragged nap of calluses catching on my soft skin in a rough caress.

He dips his head and kisses me deeper. I open to him, inviting him to give me more. We fall back into each other as easily as if we were born to do it.

His dick probes my entrance. I'm wet enough, he can push in. The stretch burns in the best way. I make a little sound and he pauses but I arch my hips up, letting him sink in a little more.

He holds himself over me, not quite all the way inside me. His broad shoulders fill my vision. All I can see is him.

"Breathe, Lainey."

I pant against his mouth. I scrape my nails down his back, scratching lightly. He's left his mark on me and I want to leave my mark on him.

Will he remember this night? Will he think of me fondly? Or will this barely be a blip on his radar; the faintest memory?

"Lainey," he calls. "Come back to me."

I blink, and study the glacier ice in his eyes. I tip my hips up and dig my nails into his back, pulling him closer. I want my skin to meld to his.

He rocks over me, moving deeper. His weight comes down on me slowly, and I breathe to better accept the pressure. Finally, he's sheathed fully inside me, his hips cradled in mine. I feel him deep in my belly. We're together as close as people can be. It's everything I've ever wanted.

"You're going to come for me again."

"I don't know if I can." I've read that it's difficult for some women to orgasm vaginally.

He pulls out a little and slides back in, angling his hips somehow so he drags over a sensitive spot in my pussy. Sparks fill my vision. "Don't think. Just feel."

His body works over mine in a rocking, easy rhythm.

"So tight," he mutters. "So beautiful. My angel."

Pressure builds in my belly. With each drag of his cock, a

hot flush comes over me and my muscles draw up tighter and tighter.

The fire's burned low but the temperature's rising. The heat builds between us.

I writhe under him, needing to move, needing more. "Joel…"

"That's it, babygirl. Say my name." He glides in and out of me. "Look at me. I'm the one who's fucking you." His cock swells inside me, stretching me until I can't take any more. "Give over, Lainey. Give everything to me."

He lowers his head and nips my lip. The combination of the pain, his scent, the way his cock rubs me—it's too much. Something inside me snaps, and golden warmth fills my limbs. Joel shudders over me, his cock pulsing deep inside me. For a moment, he lets his full weight press me into the bed. He kisses my brow, my right cheek, my lips. Then he pulls out and gathers me to his chest.

For a moment, we simply breathe.

There's nothing left of the fire but a few glowing embers. The sweat's cooling on my skin but I don't want to move. "Is it true? You've never had a girl up here?"

"Only you." He kisses my temple.

"I like that."

"Possessive, are you?"

"You have no idea. I've had a crush on you since high school." The darkness makes it easy to spill my secrets.

"You were too good for me in high school. Still are." He draws away and prowls naked into the kitchen. I squint but can't see what he's doing until he returns and presses something warm and wet to my sore pussy.

He cleans me up, wiping away the traces of himself. But part of him is deep inside me. When he's done, he tosses the washcloth on the floor, but doesn't return to my side.

I'm shivering. "Come back to me."

He fixes the quilt so it's covering me, and stretches out beside me. Other than a few pops and crackles from the dying fire, it's so quiet, I imagine I can hear the falling snow. Joel's breathing is deep and soft, but his body is tense beside me. What is he thinking?

"Joel?"

"I'm here, babygirl." But he sounds distant.

"Did… did I do okay?"

He rolls to me, gathering me in his arms. "You did perfect. You are perfect."

I settle back against him. This is what I've wanted for so long—to be in Joel's arms.

"I have a confession of my own to make," he says. "I don't need to buy groceries half as much as I do."

I knew it! I smile into the darkness. "I was wondering what you were doing with all that ground chuck."

"Sometimes I'll just drop it off at the soup kitchen. Whenever my day's too long and grinding me down, I drive past Gemma's store. And if I drive past, I have to go in. Because nothing in my life goes so wrong that it can't be fixed by seeing you."

I hum and snuggle closer. "After prison, why did you come back to town?"

"Because I was done searching for what I already had. You make your life and your happiness."

Exactly. I trail my fingers over his skin. I can't see them in the dark, but I know he has some freckles here and there. I've studied him for so long but I barely know him. It'll take me a lifetime to educate myself about this man.

"I wish…" His voice cracks.

"What?"

"I wish I could spend every night like this."

"But we can."

"No. I'm not in your plans, babygirl." His fingers stroke

my belly. "You're going to finish school and move on to bigger and better things."

"Working at a library isn't necessarily bigger and better."

"You're too smart for this town, too smart for me."

"You're plenty smart."

"Lainey, please." He catches my hand, stilling it. "I have to let you go."

"Do you want to let me go?"

"I want to hold on forever." His hand flexes, gripping my fingers tighter before releasing them. "But I have to do what's best for you."

I decide what's best for me, I want to say. Instead, I look out the window. The snow's mostly stopped falling. A few errant flakes drift through the dark blue square. "What time is it?"

I feel him shrug. "Probably after midnight."

"So it's Christmas."

"Yes."

I got my wish. It's time to make a new one. I yawn, fighting off a rush of tiredness. It will be so nice to fall asleep in Joel's arms. It'll be a dream come true. But I want a few more moments to savor it. "Thank you for my gift."

He drops a kiss on my bare shoulder before tucking the blanket over it. "This was the best gift anyone's ever given me. I'll never forget this."

He makes it sound so final. And now I understand: he doesn't think he deserves me. *Oh, Joel.* "You think I'm smart, right?"

"Smartest one I know."

"Then trust I know what I want."

"Lainey—"

"It'll work out."

His sigh stirs my hair, but he doesn't argue. "Go to sleep."

Obedient as ever, I relax against him.

You make your life and your happiness.

Joel thinks we can't last. He thinks that when the sun comes up and the snow stops falling, he'll have to let me go.

But there is magic on Christmas. Maybe it'll be enough to work another miracle.

So I close my eyes, and make another wish.

EPILOGUE

ONE YEAR LATER...

oel

I SWING the ax above my head and let it fall. The log splits with a satisfying thunk. The temperature's falling below freezing. My breath is white on the wind but the work warms my muscles until I'm sweating and tempted to strip down to my shirt sleeves. I'm almost done, and it's a good thing—the clouds overhead tell me a blizzard's on its way.

I hustle to chop the rest of the wood, setting aside the best pieces to sell online. Turns out woodworkers will pay premium dollar for New Hampshire hardwood. I spent the last year building up my online shop, finding the best wood and planting trees to replace what I've cut down. Between that and the jobs I get fixing cars, it's been a good year. I made enough to add a room to the cabin, and that's a good thing too, because I'm not the only one living here now, and we need the room.

The snow's starting to fall when the door swings open

and Lainey steps out. The sight of her makes me catch my breath, the same as it always does. The same as it did years ago, when I came back to town and she greeted me with a shy, soft voice in the grocery store.

Her cheeks curve, pink where the cold nips them, and her smile lights up the gray day.

"There he is," she coos to the little bundle in her arms. "There's Daddy."

"It's too cold to be outside."

"He wants you," she says, tipping the bundle to show me my son's tiny face. He has blue eyes the exact color of mine, but his round cheeks and angelic smile are all Lainey.

"Go inside. I'm almost done."

She obeys. The door shuts but I can still hear her talking to Joel Junior, singing a lullaby off-key.

I savor the sound. It's been one year since she trekked up here to give me the most precious gift anyone's ever given me. A gift that keeps giving. Our son was born in September. We got married in June, after Lainey graduated. She got a part-time job in a nearby college town, and helps me with the store on the side.

Lainey thinks there's magic on Christmas, but I have another theory. There's nothing supernatural about my wife's determination and a car that won't stop breaking down. It's Lainey.

She's the magic.

Thank you, I mouth to the frozen air. To whoever's listening: God or angels or just the snow-filled clouds in the sky. *Thank you.*

I set my ax under a tarp and head back inside to my home and my wife and my son. My angel, my redemption.

My miracle.

The End

***

117

Author's note,

Yay, Lainey & Joel (and baby makes three)! I know these stories are short but I hope they're satisfying.

If you want more lumberjacks, check out Beauty and the Lumberjacks, available free at https://geni.us/8lumberjacks. :D

—Lee

REVENGE IS SWEET

"Did you think, for a minute, I might want to be awake for the proposal?" I ask, fluttering my fingers so the huge princess cut diamond on my hand catches the light.

His eyes go soft and warm. "I couldn't risk you running again.

There's a tracking device in there."

"Tracking device?" I squeak, when I find my voice.

"Oh yes," he murmurs. "You will not escape me again."

***

The minute I walked into her bakery I knew Leah was destined to be my wife.

A mafia prince takes what he wants. She doesn't know who I am, or the depths of my obsession with her.

But she will.

This Valentine's day, I will make her mine.

Reviews:

"Luscious Like Eating A Freshly Baked Muffin"

"A bada$$ mafioso who believes in fate and destiny... willing to do anything to keep Leah safe and in his life forever...Pink cupcakes for the win!"

"A fairytale come true. Definitely 5 plus stars!"

DEDICATION

Dedicated to all the curvy girls who are great at baking and deserve love even when we burn the occasional dishcloth.

Also Nanette, who is a cookie and chocolate goddess. You deserve to have your own tall, dark, mafia man steal you away.

A big thank you to Ines Johnson for a fabulous beta and sensitivity read. You deserve all the chocolate!

And special thanks to the Goddess Group, who helped with the poll to choose a fun title. Here are all the titles that got a lot of votes but didn't win:

- *Death & Cupcakes*
- *"Revenge is a dish best served with Chocolate Sprinkles"*
- *"Bullets, Blood & Blonde Brownies"*
- *"Bullets and Buttercream"*
- *"GUNS & SCONESES"*
- *"There's a Chocolate Horse Head in my Bed"*
- *"Say hello to my little... flan"*
- *Keep your Friends close and your Eclairs Closer"*

Join Lee Savino's Goddess Group on Facebook or follow me on Tiktok for more wacky fun.

CHAPTER 1

The sun's just waking up as I trudge from the bus stop through piles of matted and dirty snow. On this gray February morning, there's only one shop whose windows are lit up in the dark and rundown strip mall. Even with the scuffed and faded pale pink paint, the bakery is a cheery and welcoming sight.

The door sticks, but when I lean my weight into it, it stutters open and sets the overhead bell jingling merrily. My mouth begins watering a second before the caramel and cinnamon scents hit me in a blast of warmth.

Heaven is a bakery ten minutes before opening. Specifically, Panetteria Principessa, the best bakery in my hometown, Dumont, and possibly all of the world. It doesn't matter that my cheap boots are soggy or that my cheeks are chapped with cold. It's gonna be a good day.

"Good morning," I trill, stomping my feet to shake off the crust of dirty ice. The shop is warm and smells like cinnamon buns. The scent gives me a sugar rush.

"*Buongiorno*, Leah!" Mr. Rossi shouts from the back, glee radiating through his tone. "Come see what I have done!"

"One sec." I turn and yank on the door handle, making the bell dance and ring again and again. "The door is sticking." Cold air leaks through the cracks.

"I will fix it later. You must come and see!"

"You're gonna pay a ton in heating costs," I warn, but I give up tugging and stroll further into the shop.

"I already do." Mr. Rossi sounds cheerful, but I wince. Heating bills suck. It's not like we can keep the front door closed. Every new customer will bring in an unwelcome blast of winter.

It's a good day to bake, if only to keep the oven on.

The front cases are already filled with chocolate muffins and red velvet cupcakes topped with the most perfect pillowy frosting. A few steps past the counter is the doorway to the back. There's no door, and when I step through, I'm embraced by the yeasty scent of cinnamon rolls and the bright citrus scent of lemon poppy seed muffins.

I'm so lucky to work in my favorite place in the world.

To the left are all the ovens, giving off delicious heat. I tug off my thin coat and unwind my cream-colored scarf. Underneath my winter things, I'm wearing a soft pink sweater that makes my brown skin glow. The knit fabric would be too hot to work in if I were back here all day, but as I'm alternating between the front and the back, it will be perfect.

In the corner, Mr. Rossi's head sticks out from a row of huge shiny cylinders sitting on an ornate metal box—some sort of machine I've never seen before.

"Ahh, there she is!" His weathered face splits into a smile. "Descending like an angel from heaven."

I chuckle and shed my matching cream mittens and hat. There's nothing flirtatious about my boss's exuberance. He's a sweetheart to everyone. Besides, he's madly in love with his wife.

"You must come see!" he cries, waving his hands in joy. A thin fringe of dark curls bounces around his otherwise bald pate. Light reflects between both the pale patch of bare skin on the top of his head and the metal antique that dominates the corner of the room. "I have found the answer to all our troubles."

The answer to all our troubles is a metallic monstrosity, sitting on a cart. It's taller than I am, with three cylindrical turrets on the top of a brass box.

"What is it?"

"*Una macchina per caffè espresso.* Very vintage. Very rare. I have finally found it! The machine that will turn beans into gold!"

"This is the espresso machine?" When Mr. Rossi told me he was bidding on one at an auction, I was excited. But I was not expecting this. "How old is it?"

"Thirty, forty years… but it works fine."

Oh God. This thing is older than I am.

Mr. Rossi must not see my expression, because he continues. "Cappuccino, latte, *il caffe*—it makes it all. Soon, we will be printing money!"

I hide my sigh. I've heard this before. I can only hope this time, it's true. "What did Cedella say?"

"She has not seen it yet." His face falls. "Only a picture. She can't do stairs, not today."

Mrs. Rossi—Cedella—has the swollen joints of advanced rheumatoid arthritis. Today must be one of her bad days. The cold makes her body ache so bad, she mostly stays in bed.

"I'll make her favorite scones today," I announce. "Maybe by then we'll have this working and we can make her a latte —she can be the first to try a cup."

"Yes." He brightens. "Thank you, Leah. You are an angel.

Soon, she will be better." He grabs a rag and starts polishing the machine.

"Did you look into the infusion treatments?" I ask. "I hear the results are almost miraculous."

"Yes, yes, just need a bit more money for that. But that is where this comes in…" He gives the machine another swipe. "A little beans, a little water, and we will be printing money!"

"Right." I hate to be the voice of reason, but someone has to be. Mrs. Rossi is usually around to ground her husband after his flights of fancy, but she's stuck upstairs, so it'll have to be me. "Um… does it work?"

"Of course! Just needs a little bit of polish." With a final swipe, Mr. Rossi tosses aside the rag and rubs his hands together. "Good as new. Help me move it, darling girl."

Mr. and Mrs. Rossi took me under their wing and gave me a job when I was fifteen and in foster care. Now, I make enough to live on my own even though money is tight. For them, I would do anything.

It takes both of us to roll the machine out, and by the time we've lifted the heavy monstrosity off the cart and onto a clear section at the very end of the side counter, I'm sweating, and my sweater is smudged with the last bit of dust. I have to admit, the machine looks very fancy.

"*Perfetto*," Mr. Rossi announces. "Now we will be printing money!"

"As soon as we learn to use it," I remind him. "Is there an instruction manual?"

"Not that I know of." Mr. Rossi rubs his head until his curls spring up in a childish halo.

"That's okay," I say. The original manual was probably written in Chaucer's English. Or an obscure Italian dialect. "I'll figure it out." I pat the machine, and something falls off the back with a clang. I snatch my hand back.

"We will be printing money!" Mr. Rossi dashes to the

back and returns with a stack of the white paper cups we use for the drip coffee. He's so excited, he drops a few cups on the floor, and they promptly roll under the counter.

Mr. Rossi scrambles around the counter and crouches in front of the chalkboard sign we use as a menu.

"Um, maybe we should wait until we've figured out how —" I start, but he's already adding the word *Lattes* in a barely legible scrawl underneath the usual list of coffee, tea, and daily muffin flavor.

Guess we're making lattes now.

"Do we have enough milk?" I ask, coming to stand next to him. "Because lattes require milk."

"Oh. No." Mr. Rossi scratches his head.

"All right." I carefully erase what he's written and write out *Espresso* in my neat script. "Let's start small." I frown at the espresso maker. "Are you sure there's no instruction manual? Maybe a Latin scroll, handwritten by monks?"

Mr. Rossi has already disappeared into the back. He comes back out carrying a box filled with several shiny pieces, and lengths of opaque plastic hosing. "I forgot to reattach these," he says and ducks his head like a little boy with his hand caught in the biscotti jar.

The oven buzzer blares.

"Okay." I take the box of missing and probably essential espresso machine parts. "I'll deal with this. You deal with the oven—leave the muffins out, and I'll fill the case once they're cool. Then you can go check on Cedella." I'll try to figure the machine out while he's upstairs and out of my hair.

"*Perfetto.*" Mr. Rossi salutes me and scurries off, leaving me grinning. Sometimes my boss just needs to be told what to do.

"Tell her I'll be making the apricot and cream cheese scones! They're her favorite," I call after him.

"*Sei un angelo!*" *You're an angel!*

"Too bad I'm not an engineer," I mutter to the box of missing parts in my hand before setting it aside. Maybe the bad weather will make the morning rush light, and I'll have time to figure out the glossy monstrosity on the countertop.

* * *

WITH SNOW MIXED with sleet spitting from the clouds outside, I expected fewer morning customers, but the popularity of my muffins proves me wrong.

The lemon poppy seed ones run out first, like they always do, followed by the cinnamon buns.

Mr. Rossi returns and helps at the counter while I whip up a big batch of Mrs. Rossi's favorite scones, and do a quick check in case there's an espresso machine instruction manual lying around that Mr. Rossi forgot about.

So far, the coffee shop gods have smiled on us and everyone ordered their usual—a drip coffee and a muffin. But in between customers, Mr. Rossi reminds me that "We are going to be on the map! We will be printing money!" so he's probably not going to give up on the machine any time soon. That means I need to become a barista, stat.

In my search, I unearth an old Italian cookbook, and tuck it under my arm to take out front and read between customers. Mr. Rossi pretty much lets me bake whatever I want, and I've been wanting to try some new recipes. Why not biscotti to go with the espresso?

When the morning rush is over, I make a cup of mint tea and hand it to Mr. Rossi. "Why don't you bring that up to the missus?"

"Oh, she'll love that. Thank you, Leah." He beams and disappears, leaving me in an empty shop. I putter around and tidy up, savoring the quiet.

The bakery is my favorite place in the world, but I especially love it before opening, or in the break between the morning and lunch time rushes. That's when I get a chance to bake.

Other than that, I wouldn't change anything about the bakery—except maybe the tip jar with the handmade label taped to it. Last summer, Mr. Rossi scrawled *Leah's College Fund* on it. Totally embarrassing when my fellow high school students were coming in for their morning coffee, especially my cheating ex and his new, beautiful, blonde and scrawny prom queen of a girlfriend. Now that it's February and they're back at their fancy Ivy league college, I can breathe a little easier.

I like my little life. I wouldn't change anything—except the lack of funds in my or Mr. Rossi's bank account. And getting better medicine for Mrs. Rossi.

I'm in the back, sifting confectioner's sugar to make a quick almond-flavored glaze for the cooling scones, when the bell jingles.

"Coming," I call. My grip on the sugar bag slips and a

white cloud puffs in my face. I grab a wet cloth and pat my face before rushing out to help the customer.

A tall man in a long, black pea coat is standing in front of the counter, his dark glossy head bent towards me as he regards the chalkboard menu. My steps slow. I have the strangest sensation, like I'm about to step over a threshold to another world. I'm holding my breath.

He raises his head, and my heart trips over itself. Strong jaw, dark olive skin, patrician nose—his face is beautiful, regal, and unapproachable all at the same time.

I take a step forward and my elbow knocks over a stack of the paper to-go cups. I fumble to catch them, but only manage to kick them, sending them rolling across the floor. Now I'm bobbing and weaving up and down, trying to catch them all.

Is it too much to hope the handsome customer didn't notice? I look up and he's leaning over the counter, his dark eyes on me. His beautiful lips twitch. "Need help?"

Lordy, his voice is as beautiful as his face. Smooth and deep. Delicious.

"I'm all right," I say. Reaching up, I try to set a stack of cups back on the counter, but miss it entirely and they all fall back down. One bonks me on the head.

"Never mind," I say, rising and taking my place behind the register. I heroically ignore the fallen cups littering the floor at my feet. "What can I get you?" I dust my hands off briskly. Calm, professional. That's the ticket.

"*Un espresso*," he says in a delicious bass that sends goose-bumps flowing up my arms. My very floury arms. Crap, I'm covered in flour. And powdered sugar. And some cinnamon. I surreptitiously try to brush some off, but there are still little white and reddish brown flecks dusting my hands.

"An espresso?" I repeat. "We don't—"

The man's gaze swings to my right, and I turn to follow it

to the antique espresso maker sitting on the counter. The machine gleams, silently judging my lack of barista skills. "Oh, right."

The bell rings again and three more guys walk in. They're all wearing dark coats and have the same dark and gorgeous Mediterranean features as the first guy. Are Dolce and Gabbana doing a photoshoot outside?

The four guys look so similar, if they're not brothers, they've got to be cousins. The first one at the counter staring at me is the most beautiful of them all. And he's still got his whole attention on me, looking like he's hungry and I'm a sugar-dusted donut.

My blush starts at my nipples and starts rolling slowly up my cleavage—which is on display. Thanks to the heat of the ovens, I peeled off my sweater and am only wearing a white camisole. And tomorrow's laundry day, so I'm down to my last, most ridiculous lacy bra. Pink, of course. Luckily, the cami is thick enough to conceal everything, but the bright straps are showcased on my shoulders. The blast of cold air that tailed the customers makes my nipples spring to points.

"Right," I say. "I'll just get you that, then..." I turn and knock another cup off the counter. This one I catch and clutch carefully as I walk over to my new nemesis. My expression, mirrored in the polished chrome, is full of dismay. I hope the customer can't see my reflection.

The three domes on top are like miniature replicas of St. Peter's basilica. Ornate and just as intimidating. One dome is labeled: *Cappuccino.*

"A cappuccino?" I ask, reaching for the level hopefully.

"No, *principessa.* Only an espresso."

Rats.

Between customers this morning, Mr. Rossi and I figured out how to turn this thing on. I push a button and jump as steam hisses out. Maybe there is a steamer attachment—good for steaming milk.

"Whoops," I say. "Not that one." I pull out the metal thingy, add the freshly ground beans, and tamp them down. I wedge the metal thingy holding the espresso grounds back in and push a different button. A green light comes on.

Then the entire machine starts shaking like it's going to blast off of the countertop. It's the espresso-making cousin of Howl's Moving Castle.

"We just got this espresso maker," I shout cheerfully over my shoulder. I keep my face calm, as if everything is normal. *Fake it till you make it.*

The men by the door smirk at each other, but the man at the front still hasn't taken his eyes off me. There's a prickle on the back of my neck when I turn.

"Come on, come on," I murmur to the machine. "You can do it."

Just when I've given up hope, there's a hiss, and a squirt of unappetizing brown liquid into the paper cup. It smells sort of coffee-ish.

Thanking the coffee shop gods for their continued good favor, I take the paper cup back to the customer and set it in front of him. The four men in front of the counter regard it.

"I'm more of a tea person, really," I say to fill the silence. My blush has reached the crests of my cheeks and is in the process of unfurling like twin red flags in front of a bull.

The beautiful man says nothing but picks up the cup and, with more bravery than I've seen in a long time, tosses it back. The room is still as he slowly sets the cup back down.

"It's good," he lies through his teeth.

I wrinkle my nose at him.

"Looks like brown water," one of his friends jokes, and something in the man's dark brown eyes goes icy. From nice and amiable to full of cold anger. His jaw clenches. "Out," he orders without turning.

To my surprise, the men on either side of him—his brothers or cousins or whatever—straighten, and march out the door. The bell jingles in their wake.

I gulp a breath, meeting the beautiful man's gaze. It's us alone in the room. Just me, and the man I served sad brown water.

"I'm sorry," I say, gesturing to the evil machine. "It's brand new… well, brand new to us. We just got it, and a couple of the pieces fell off." I reach down, grab the box, and show him the contents.

He leans over to study the box of parts. A pause, and he nods. "Right."

To my surprise, he swings off his coat and lays it on the counter. His friends are still waiting outside the door, their backs to the bakery. One blows on his fingers as if to warm them, but they seem content to stand outside the shop. As ordered.

Weird.

The beautiful man has gone to the door and flipped the 'Open' sign to 'Closed.'

"What are you doing?" I squeak.

"Making an espresso," he says, catching my gaze and holding it as he undoes his onyx and silver cufflinks. He sets them down and rolls up the sleeves of his luxurious dress shirt.

Why is he undressing? Not that I'm complaining.

He keeps talking, his smooth voice rich as espresso. Well-made espresso.

"*Mia zia* had a machine like this," he says. "It broke and I fixed it. I'm good at fixing things. It made me her favorite nephew." His right cheek creases for a moment and I catch sight of a dimple. Goodness gracious. Model stunning looks and then a dimple.

I go to fan myself and knock over another paper cup.

"Sorry," I mumble. "Durn things… always in the way."

The beautiful man is behind the counter now. I don't know what's happening, but I do know his dark eyes are the color of bitter chocolate.

"You have sugar…" He holds my eyes as he gestures to my front, and I look down in horror. I've gotten powdered sugar all over my front. My breasts look like the snow-speckled twin peaks of Mount Kilimanjaro.

"Oh!" I try to dust it off and end up smearing sugar everywhere. Now my breasts just look glazed.

The customer tilts his head. He's looking into my eyes, not at my breasts. I'll give him points for that. "Allow me," he mutters, nodding his head towards the espresso maker.

On autopilot, I step out of the way. There's something about him that makes me want to follow his orders. Or maybe I just want to study him from the back.

And what a sexy backside he has. A firm ass in sleek black slacks. There's a hint of expensive cologne swirling around me. Not too much, not unpleasant. I lean in closer before I realize I'm sniffing him.

Luckily, he doesn't notice. He takes the box and approaches the recalcitrant machine. Implements clatter as he starts removing and reattaching random tubes and metal protrusions. I hover at his shoulder, my hands helpless at my sides.

"You don't have to do this," I say. "Your friends are outside…" The three men are standing on the snowy sidewalk, their hands shoved in the pockets of their dark coats. They look bored and cold.

"They'll wait," he says, and bangs on the side of the machine so hard, I jump.

"Easy, *principessa*," he murmurs. *Principessa* means *princess*. I know that much from working here.

What I don't know is why he's calling me 'princess.' Or why my fingers are itching to bury themselves in the stranger's thick, black hair.

"This is Stefanos' territory," he says while he works. "Does he give you any trouble?"

"I don't think so…" Stefanos? Have I heard that name before? "Mr. Rossi owns the building, so there's no landlord."

"Hmm." He pauses in his work to reach into a pocket, and hands me a black business card. "If you have any trouble, you call me."

Okaaay. I study the card. 'Royal Regis' is all it says, along with a single number. A cell number?

"Royal Royal," I say, because *Regis* means something like *royal* in Latin.

"Yes?" His lip crooks upward, giving me a flash of white teeth.

"That's your name?"

"My parents had high hopes." He shrugs. His hair flops in his face and gives him a boyish look. "And you are Leah."

"What?" I say, startled that he knows my name. He must have read it on the damn tip jar. "Um, yes."

"Lovely," he says softly, before returning to work. I blush all over again.

A few minutes later, he's re-arranged the levers and reattached the missing hoses, all while I mostly stood around and ogled his ass.

Then he tugs me in front of him, positioning me at the machine with him at my back. He's big, much bigger than I am. The sleek lines of his suit disguised his broad shoulders, but I feel them as he reaches around me, guiding my hand in the correct pattern. First, we put fresh grounds in the metal thingy and then attach it to the correct spot. His hand is warm on mine. His fresh cologne surrounds me, blending with the scent of the coffee grounds.

"Now, Leah," he orders, and a thrill runs up my spine. His breath warms the back of my neck.

"This button," he instructs, pressing it with me. "And pull this." We pull the lever together. "*E presto...*"

The machine hums—nothing like last time's shuddering dramatics. A rich brown fluid shoots out and fills the cup. It smells divine.

He holds my eyes as he takes the cup and sips. "*Perfetto,*" he pronounces. Still looking right at me, he presses the cup to my lips. "Taste," he orders. My mouth opens. I'm not really a coffee person, but the smooth liquid is dark and sinful on my tongue.

"Oh," I breathe. "That's good."

"*Si.*" We're standing so close together, our faces are inches apart.

"How did you do that?" I whisper like we're trading secrets.

"I have a way with women," he says. "She's a woman, no?"

"Sure," I agree, because I'd agree with anything he says.

"Beautiful women just need to be touched the right way. And I am an expert." He looks at me through his long black lashes.

Is he flirting? With me?

Naw. "Yes, well, it makes sense," I blurt. "You're very handsome." I clap a hand over my mouth so I stop talking, and back up until I bump into the counter. The rest of the cups fall and bounce off the floor.

Oh well. I'll tell Mr. Rossi to take the cost of the cups out of my pay.

A slow smile spreads across his face. He looks like the devil about to make a deal. "You've got some sugar right there." He points to my cheek. I rub the back of my hand over my cheek. My blush makes my skin hot to the touch, like I have roasting coals in my face.

"Here." He slowly raises a hand and swipes his thumb across my cheek. Holding my gaze, he licks his thumb. "Sweet," he says.

"Thank you," I say. I'm not sure why my brain has completely scampered out the door. *Say something!* "So… your aunt liked espresso?"

"Mmm." He looks amused, like he knows I'm fumbling for something to continue our conversation. "But not for breakfast. She liked tea—like you. Every morning, she'd have a cup, and into it she would dip *un biscotto.* A cookie."

"Biscotti!" I brighten. Cookies, I can talk about. Cookies, I know. "I was going to make a few of those for the espresso. And…" I snatch up the cookbook. "There's another cookie here that looks interesting." I flip through the sauce-spattered pages until I find the right recipe. "Chocolate and hazelnut…"

"*Strazzate,*" he says at the same time as I try to pronounce the Italian word and butcher it.

"*Strazzate,*" I repeat, trying to trill the 'r' and give the word the same melodic lilt that he gave it. "It sounds delicious."

The words catch in my throat as I glance at him. He's leaning over me now, hands planted on the counter top on either side of me, head close to mine. The cookbook is sandwiched between us, pressing against my boobs. "If you make me *strazzate,*" he murmurs into my ear while the hair on my neck rises, "I will marry you."

Oh dear. My hand trembles and there's a loud rip. "Oh dear," I say out loud. I've completely torn the recipe out of the book. RIP, page forty-three. I turn slowly and he moves back to give me space—but not much. "I guess I'll have to make it now." I wave the torn scrap of the recipe between us like a white flag of surrender.

Royal's looking at me like I'm a cookie he wants to take a bite out of. "*Mia zia* told me if I ever found a woman who is beautiful and bakes *strazzate*, I should make her my wife."

I scrunch my nose. "That's not a very high criterion, is it?"

He chuckles. "It is harder to find such a woman than you might think."

"Well, I'm sure you'll find someone," I chirp. "It *is* specific… you could put it on your dating profile."

Royal shakes his head and gently tugs the recipe out of my hand.

"You make these, Leah, I'll make you my wife."

Oh, I do like my name on his tongue.

"Shouldn't be hard," I whisper.

His chuckle is rich and dark. My toes curl.

"It'll be easy. I just need chocolate, almonds…" *his dark head bowed close to mine.*

"Do you have Strega?" he asks softly.

"No, but I could order it…"

"I will have some sent to you." He lifts my hand and presses a kiss to it. "Until tomorrow, *principessa*."

He sweeps out from behind the counter. My legs are so weak, one wobble, and I'd be on the floor with the fallen cups.

On his way out, he pauses to remove something from his sleek black wallet and slot it into the tip jar.

Then he's gone, leaving me to shuffle through the sea of white cups back to the counter.

He left a hundred in the tip jar.

CHAPTER 2

The next morning, I blow in with a wintry wind before five a.m. There's a bottle of Strega on the countertop, sitting on the ripped scrap of paper that holds the recipe.

"Mr. Rossi?" I call. "Did you leave this here?"

"No, I thought you left it." He sidles up to Big Bernadette, as I have named the espresso maker, inspired by Royal's *she's a woman, no?* comment. "You got the machine working!"

"Um, sorta." With a lot of help from a gorgeous customer.

"Soon, we will be printing money! And look," he holds up the tip jar, "one hundred seventeen dollars, for your college fund." He beams before disappearing into the back.

"Yay." I pick the scrap of paper up. "*Strazzate.*" I try the word out, mimicking Royal's lilting pronunciation.

If you make me strazzate, Royal said, *I will marry you.*

I drop the card with a shiver. Somehow, Royal got me a bottle of Strega for the authentic recipe. Either that, or little Italian fairies delivered it.

I bet I'll get a Royal visit later today. I could make the cookies… and text him? His card is burning a hole in my pocket, but after the morning rush, I have my college class. If I text him, he'll know when to come.

That's the plan then. I tuck Royal's business card back in my pocket where it will keep my phone company until the appointed time. My heart is skipping as I head back to start on a batch of cinnamon rolls.

* * *

ROYAL

THE LITTLE BAKER rushes around the small space behind the counter, making espresso and filling orders. Every so often, I think she's going to finally look up and see me watching her through the front windows, but she never does. She's totally focused on the customer in front of her, giving them one hundred percent of her generous smile.

"You're watching her again," Enzo mutters at my back. "It's been every week for a year. She doesn't even know it."

"Does the prey know the hunter?" I murmur absently. I

didn't expect Leah to recognize me yesterday. It had been a year since I last entered her place of work, after all.

Enzo shakes his head. "Enough already."

When it comes to Leah, I'll never get enough. She got my gift, but she hasn't called or texted. Maybe she's too busy.

Maybe's she's afraid.

Enzo takes my silence to mean he can keep blabbing. "Just ask her out. You know she'll say yes." He lights a cigarette.

My fingers itch for a cigarette of my own, but I've quit. New year, new me. My aunt looked me in the eye as she dealt the cards. *This is the year you claim it all.*

"I don't date."

"Then ask her to fuck." Enzo blows smoke. "No woman's turned you down before." His smirk fades when I turn and he sees my expression. He raises his hands. "No offense."

I turn back to the bakery. Today, Leah looks tired, but she's pointed her megawatt smile towards a customer.

When it comes to Leah, I don't want a date. I don't want a fuck. I want so much more. "This isn't about a fuck," I say. "This is fate."

Enzo rolls his eyes, but he's smart enough not to say anything.

They don't understand, mia zia said. *But you do.* That's why I'm the chosen one.

"Your father won't like it."

I say nothing. My father's likes and dislikes don't matter to me. They haven't for a long time. If *La Famiglia* thinks they can control me through him, they're in for a nasty surprise.

Enzo knows this. He tries again, making a show of looking around. "Stefanos has men close by. You know he knows you're here. He's watching."

"So?"

"This is his territory. He's playing nice, out of respect for your father. But soon, he'll make a move..." Enzo's words fade as I turn back to the bakery again. Leah's forehead is pinched. I'm standing too far away for her to see. Does she know how long I've been watching her? Does she sense it?

It's been a year of watching, waiting, setting up the dominos. Soon, it'll be time to flick one over and let them all fall.

"Are you listening, Royal?" Enzo says. He's my second in command, but he knows nothing of the plans I've made. No one does.

"No," I reply. "But I heard you. Stefanos doesn't like me hanging around."

Enzo puffs his cigarette more rapidly. "He'll make a move."

I shove my hands in my pockets. "Then it's time we make ours."

"Seriously?" Enzo tosses the cigarette into the snow. I'm already striding away.

"Yes. Today," I tell him. By tonight, I'll have everything I want. My kingdom, my throne. But every king needs a queen.

This is the year you claim it all. Starting with her.

* * *

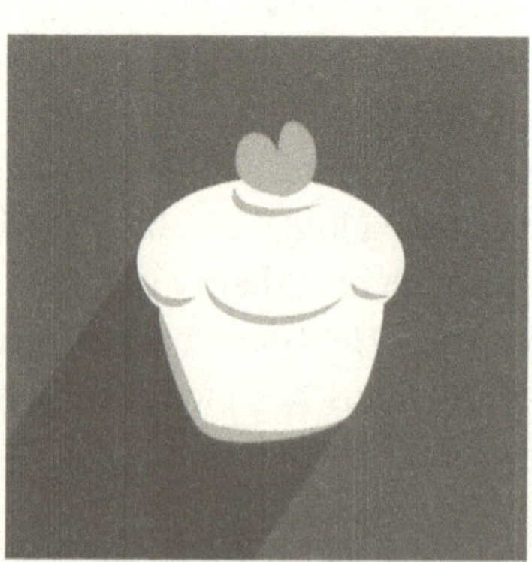

LEAH

THIS MORNING IS OFFICIALLY a dumpster fire. Nothing goes right. An oven breaks, a timer doesn't go off and I burn a batch of lemon poppyseed muffins—and of course our best customers are all disappointed that their favorite is out of stock.

The morning rush is more frantic than usual but Mrs. Rossi is doing so poorly, Mr. Rossi has to stay upstairs to help her for half an hour at a time.

Then one of my former friends from high school walks in. I say former because Piper only hung around me because of my popular boyfriend. Until he dumped me.

"Oh, Leah, it's you," she says. Her backpack and sweatshirt are both branded with a Princeton logo. "I didn't realize you still worked here." She glances at the chalkboard menu. "I'll have a grande Americano."

Wrong bougie coffeeshop. I bite my tongue until it pinches to keep from snapping at her. After she pays, I dump regular coffee into a regular sized cup—we only have one size. Most Americans can't tell a drip coffee from a watered-down espresso.

When I set Piper's order in front of her, she glances up from her phone. "Are you still in touch with Josh?"

"No."

"He's at Empire University now, right?" She shifts her weight, straightening her Princeton backpack.

"I think so." With his new girlfriend.

"K. See ya." Piper takes the cup and trots off. I stomp to the back to take out my frustration on the dirty baking bowls soaking in the sink.

Mr. Rossi pops his head into the bakery. "Doing all right, Leah?"

I swallow a sharp response. It's not Mr. Rossi's fault he's had to help his wife all morning and leave me with the morning rush. Nor is it his fault my ex-friend Piper dropped in and made me feel two inches tall.

"All good here." I force my tone to be light.

"*Sei un angelo.*" The stress falls from Mr. Rossi's voice. It takes a toll on him—his wife's condition. There are dark circles under his eyes but he wears a tired smile. "I haven't forgotten you have class today. Cedella still needs me but I'll be back down soon, okay?"

"Okay." I mash my lips into something that's more smile than frown.

"You making the pink cupcakes?"

"No," I say warily. "Should I?"

"You always make them for Valentine's Day."

Right, it's almost Valentine's Day. The worst holiday ever invented by the American candy and greeting card industry. Last year, my boyfriend dumped me the day before, and stopped by on February fourteenth to pick up coffee for himself and his new girlfriend. "Pink cupcakes. Right. I'll get started on those when I get back, okay?"

"*Va bene,*" Mr. Rossi says distractedly, and ducks out of the bakery again.

So much for making *strazzate* today. It's not like Royal would be back anyway, even if I called him.

Why would he want to?

Happy endings aren't for a girl like me.

LEAH

ON THE WAY back from class, my boots are soggy again. I really need to replace them, but I also have to pay my phone bill and rent. Then I have college tuition, which is way more than a hundred and seventeen dollars a credit.

Why am I even bothering with college? At this point it'll take me seventy-five years to graduate, and several lifetimes to pay off the debt.

When the pale pink store front is in view, I try to shake my sadness. Why am I feeling like this? It's not because I'm single. It's not because I'm working at a bakery. It's because when I add up the pieces of my life, the total sum equals pathetic.

Is this what my life is going to be like?

I'm so caught up in thoughts, I'm almost at the bakery when I realize the Closed sign is flipped and the lights are off, but the door is half cracked.

That's odd. Maybe Mrs. Rossi took a turn for the worse and Mr. Rossi didn't want to have to deal with any customers.

I walk in and carefully close the door behind me so as not

to let the heat out. Something crunches under my cheap boots. Glass.

I turn and gasp. The front cases are smashed. Broken glass covers the floor and countertop. Glinting shards coat the remaining cupcakes and muffins. Big Bernadette is lying on her side on the floor, dented. Coffee's pooled on the floor, looking like black blood.

"Mr. Rossi," I cry. There's a faint groan from the kitchen area. I fly over the shattered glass to the back.

Mr. Rossi is crumpled in a corner, surrounded by the pots, pans, and whisks littering the floor. I race through the piles of spilled flour to crouch at his side.

"Leah, he groans. The skin around his eyes is bruised. His cheek is red and swelling. "I tried to call you," he mumbles through swollen lips. "Tell you not to come in."

"Easy." I take his arm gingerly, wincing when he does, and help him sit up. We both stare at the wreckage of the bakery. "What happened?"

"Stefanos came."

"Stefanos? Who is Stefanos?" Where have I heard that name before?

"Said I owed him."

"What? I thought you owned the place."

"Not rent. Protection."

"Protection," I repeat. "From whom?"

"From him. Told him I didn't have the money. They didn't take no for an answer."

"Shhh," I murmur, patting his bruised hand. He winces and I feel like an idiot. "It'll be okay. I'll get you to the hospital and then call the police—"

"No." Mr. Rossi grabs my hand and squeezes, despite his bruises. "No hospital. No police."

"But…"

"No. They're coming back."

A chill spreads through the pit of my stomach. I ignore it and say briskly, "Let's get you up and into a chair. I can get you some ice for your head—"

"No. No time. They know that she's upstairs." She. Mrs. Rossi. Bedridden. This Stefanos guy and his men just trashed the place and beat up Mr. Rossi. *They're coming back.*

Mr. Rossi coughs and clutches my hand harder. "I need a favor."

"Anything."

"Go to the safe." He points to the cupboard tucked behind the washing machine. "Now." He pushes me. "Go."

I resist. "You need a doctor."

"Don't want her to know."

"She's going to find out," I snap. This is a mess. This is a nightmare. "Fine." I rise and go to the cupboard, opening it to the safe. "What now?"

"The combination is June 21st, 1989."

Mr. and Mrs. Rossi's wedding date. I suck in a breath and turn the dial, starting with zero, six…

It clicks open, revealing stacks of cash.

"Take it all." Mr. Rossi's breath whistles a little. Did he break a rib?

"But this is your savings," I cry. "This was for her treatment." There are tears in my eyes. "You can't do this."

"I have to." Mr. Rossi chokes. More blood trickles out of his nose. "Please, Leah," he says. "You must take it to them. And be quick. I wouldn't ask you—"

"No, no, I'll do it." I stuff the money into one of our white paper bakery bags, and tuck it under my coat.

I stop at the sink on my way to the door. I can't just leave Mr. Rossi like this.

"Here." I press the wet tissue to his nose.

He raises a shaking hand to hold it. "Go now, Leah. Do

you know the office building on the other side of the fountain?"

"Yes."

"Look for number eighteen-oh-four. That is the office." His eyes are wide, the whites flashing. "Don't linger. Tell them it's for the Rossi account. Tell them it's for Stefanos."

"Stefanos. Got it."

"Leah... I'm sorry." For a moment, he looks ashamed. "I shouldn't ask you—"

"It'll be fine," I lie.

My breaths fog in my face as I stumble out of the bakery. The bell jingles, but the sound is muted against my frantic panting. Mr. Rossi's in there, mopping up his own blood. Can he move? Can he walk? I should go back and help him. Instead, I scurry past the bus stop and cross the road, maneuvering around piles of slush.

There's a twinge in my foot but I don't stop marching. Mr. Rossi mentioned a fountain. It's a ten, fifteen-minute walk.

The temperature is dropping by the minute. The sky is gray, heralding a new round of snowfall. Ice crunches under my feet. My thin coat isn't warm enough. I really need a proper winter coat, but I haven't been able to afford one. At least I have my scarf and my mittens. *And a sack full of cash.*

I hold my arms tight to my sides—so tight, my wimpy biceps are starting to ache. Stupid me didn't even think about putting the sack of cash into my purse. It's too big to stuff into any of my pockets. These leggings are old and worn and comfy but have frozen to my thighs, and the thigh pockets would barely fit a business card. I automatically reach my hand into the pockets of my coat. In the right pocket is my phone and the *strazzate* recipe torn from the cookbook. In the other... Royal's business card.

Stefanos. That's where I've heard that name before. It's the one Royal mentioned. *This is Stefanos' territory.* Stefanos, the guy who just shook Mr. Rossi down. The guy I'm supposed to deliver money to.

Does he give you any trouble? Royal had asked. Did he know something was going to happen? How would he?

I've fingered Royal's card so often, the edge is starting to curl. *If you have any trouble, you call me.* Did he mean a situation like this? Was it a warning?

My phone is dead. That's why I didn't get any of Mr. Rossi's calls. Even if it was working, would I call Royal?

What the heck is going on?

My teeth are chattering, and not just because it's cold. They clack together when I'm nervous, too. When adrenaline's soaring through my veins. At my foster home, the alarm once went off in the middle of the night, and we all stood outside on the sidewalk, waiting for my foster mom to stop the alarm from shrieking. My teeth were chattering then, even though it was the middle of summer.

They're chattering now. My morning coffee and half a burnt muffin slosh in my stomach. The fountain is ahead and beyond it, the office building. It's gray and ugly, built in a bland '70 seventies architecture style. The sort of place frequented by accountants and badly funded software star-tups. Not the sort of place I'd look to find a thug. *The banality of evil, indeed.*

There's nothing for it. I have to deliver this money. Hopefully Stefanos will accept the payment, no questions asked, and let me get on with my life. Leave Mr. Rossi alone. I can go back and get Mr. Rossi to a doctor. But the money for Mrs. Rossi's treatments, the money I'm carrying, will be gone.

I skid on the ice and nearly fall. The white bag slips out from under my arm. The top flaps open and there's a flash of green. I fall to my knees and snatch it to my chest. *Please, let no one be around.* No one to see me acting like a lunatic crossing the snowy square with a sack full of cash, trying and failing not to act like an anxious druggie rendezvousing with her dealer.

I'm still on my knees, clutching the bag to my chest with both hands, when two shiny leather brogues crunch the snow a few feet ahead of me.

A man's in front of me, his long, dark, wool coat looking blissfully warm. That's the sort of coat I need.

The scent of delicious cologne hits me, and I know who it is before I blink into the frozen wind and look up. "Royal." His name comes out with a puff of smoke.

"Where are you going, little one?"

"It's just an errand," I blurt. "For my boss." My eyes stray beyond Royal's solid form. Are those men in dark coats standing by the door marked *1804?*

Royal turns his dark head to follow my line of sight. His lips press together.

He knows. Somehow, he knows exactly why I'm here and what I'm doing. It's got to be obvious, right? I'm clutching a sack full of money.

There's frost on the edges of my lashes. I get to my feet, blinking rapidly. "Please. I need to bring this to him."

"Leah—"

"He came to the shop," I blurt.

Royal's eyes are black. "Stefanos."

I nod.

We're not alone anymore—Royal's associates are approaching the fountain. Once again, they're all in black wool coats. They look so similar, from their glossy hair to their red-tinged cheeks and hawk-like noses. Like a line of fashion models, or cousins at a family reunion, lining up for a commemorative photo.

"Leah." Royal calls my attention back to him. He comes

towards me, pulling off his expensive-looking black gloves. "I can handle it. Let me handle it." His eyes are back to a soft brown. His voice is pure sin.

He holds out his hand. I automatically start to hand him what I'm holding. Then I remember what it is. The money. *More money than I'll ever have in my life.*

"What?" he asks. His associates or cousins or whatever are watching us. I step a little closer into Royal's sphere, close enough that the heat of him emanates onto my frozen face.

"I don't even know you," I whisper.

"I know," he says. "I'm going to change that." He leans back a little, just enough that I miss the heat of him. He shrugs out of his coat and slings it around my shoulders, tucks it closed. "You shouldn't be out in this snow."

The wind blows harder. The snow's falling in wet clumps, catching on my lashes and melting on my cheeks, leaving my skin bitterly numb.

"What is it you want from me?" I can barely get the words out with my jaw clenched against the cold.

"I want to fix it," he says. *I'm good at fixing things,* he said back in the bakery.

And I don't know what it is: the gentle darkness of his eyes, the way the snowflakes caught on his long lashes, or the way he's standing in shirt sleeves with snow dusting the slopes of his shoulders—*He took off his coat for me. Again*—but I trust him.

I get that sense again, like I'm standing at a precipice, looking down. But instead of dizzy, I feel Royal's presence by my side. And I know he won't let me fall.

Surrounded by that subtle freshwater perfume, I stop thinking. Snow's frosting his black hair. He looks too beautiful to be real. But he is real, and it feels right, totally natural, to raise my hand and hand him the sack of cash.

Royal doesn't blink. He doesn't even look at the bag. In

one move, he takes it from me and hands it off to one of his clones. He snaps his fingers. "Take care of it," he orders his associates without taking his eyes off me.

The guys turn as one, and start walking towards office 1804.

"What does that mean?" I ask, staring up at Royal. "What do you mean by *take care of it?*"

"Come," he says, crowding forward. "Let's get you out of the cold."

"You mean get *you* out of the cold," I say, because I'm getting concerned. He's a big strapping man, but surely standing out here in shirtsleeves in a snowstorm is bad for him, unless he has some sort of polar bear DNA.

Royal chuckles. He's walking with me—escorting me, really—with his arm around my waist. We're heading in the opposite direction to his associates, towards a big black Escalade. He opens the back car door and bundles me into his arms, lifting me right off my feet. Inside the car the air is blissfully warm, and I half melt onto the heated leather seats.

The car door slams shut and Royal's scent fills the backseat. His big body crowds into my space. I'm scooting my butt back to make room when something cracks in the distance.

"Oh my god." I flinch, my hands flying to cover my head. I don't live in a great neighborhood and the sound of gunshots is familiar. It's different from the sound of a backfiring car.

Royal's expression changes not a bit. With another *rat-tat-tat* round of bullets sounding off in the general area of office 1804, he locks the door and nods to the driver—a big guy with a shaved head I didn't even notice before now.

More gunfire pops as the Escalade glides from the curb.

"It's okay, baby." Royal puts his arm around me. "I'll take care of you."

My teeth are chattering again.

"Let's get you out of these." He strips off my mittens and starts rubbing my stiff fingers. "Where's your winter coat?" he chides.

"I don't have one." The car's heat vents are blowing full blast. The warmth makes my skin prickle, as if my body is waking up from being so numb. It hurts. I blink back sudden tears.

"My poor angel," he says. *"Principessa mia."* He tucks my hands against him.

The Escalade has rounded a corner. The snowy square, the fountain, office 1804—they've all disappeared. With every passing second, I'm growing warmer. Relief runs through me.

"What was that back there?" I ask before I can stop myself. "The gunshots."

"Stefanos has owned this territory for a long time," Royal answers without blinking. "He won't go down without a fight."

I shrink back on the seat. Why is he telling me this?

"Don't be afraid, princess."

"I should give you your coat back." I start to squirm and shrug out of it but he stops me.

"You're still cold." He tugs the coat back onto my shoulders and tucks me into his side. "You have snow on your cheeks. In your hair." His voice rises and falls, lulling me closer. He brushes his hand over my head, and I can't help but lean into his palm. "Reminds me of sugar." He leans in and his lips brush mine. A jolt runs through me, and then a rush of heat that warms me better than the fancy heated seats.

Now I'm too hot. My heart's beating faster, a flush spreading across my face like I've just been staring into an oven.

"Where are we going?" The driver has us whizzing down

a road I don't recognize. The day has turned darker. Heavy gray clouds coat the sky.

"More snow is coming," Royal says, not answering my question. "You shouldn't be out without a winter coat."

The last of the adrenaline leaves my system, and my head droops. Something about his scent and the heat of his body makes me drowsy.

"I need to make sure that you're safe," Royal's murmuring above my head. "We're going to my place."

My eyelids are heavy as I stare ahead. The windshield wipers work overtime, swiping away thick clumps of falling snow.

My head drops to his shoulder, and I wake out of my stupor with a jerk. I almost fell asleep on him. "I'm so sorry. I need to get back to Mr. Rossi."

"I'm sending a doctor to his house."

"Okay," I say, even though I don't believe him. What real doctor would do a house call? "Did... Did Stefanos beat him up?"

"Yes." Royal's face turns to stone. "Or one of his men."

I cuddle closer even though I should be terrified out of my mind. "I don't like this," I whisper.

"I know, *bella.* But you needn't worry. I won't allow any harm to come to you. Let me make sure that you're okay."

"Okay."

His dark eyes crinkle. "Okay," he whispers back.

The sudden switch from cold to hot, the drain of adrenaline, Royal's scent—it all combines, and I fall asleep leaning against his crisp Italian dress shirt.

When I wake, we're in a hilly area outside of town. There are mansions here. A lot of them. Giant mix and match monstrosities built with no rhyme or reason into the side of the hill. We pass a Gothic Tudor style one with massive white marble statues dotting its lawn, then a Victorian style one covered in frantic gingerbread trim.

We leave the McMansions behind and head further up a mountain. Now the snowfall, which had thinned a bit, picks up speed. The driver must feel like he's in a video game of some sort, with distracting white specks flying at his screen.

We turn down a long drive lined with a thick cedar hedge. A private road, but it's better plowed than the public road before it. The SUV rolls between the hedges for what feels like a mile, and then we're turning into a large circular driveway and pulling up in front of a real mansion built of solid brick.

"What is this place?" I breathe.

"This is my home. Come." And he pulls me from the SUV.

CHAPTER 3

I must still be in a dream-like state, because Royal guides me from the SUV into the house without me stopping to argue, freak out, or even worry all that much. I'm too in awe of the place, which looks more like a hotel for billionaires than a home—much less a young man like Royal's home. How much do Dolce and Gabbana models make?

To my relief, the first place we enter is the kitchen. It's huge and warm with rich Turkish rugs on the wooden floors. Very fancy. With two ovens, it's bigger than the working space of Mr. Rossi's bakery. The marble-topped island is bigger than my bed.

"This is beautiful," I say.

"I thought you'd like it." Royal's lounging in the doorway, leaning against the frame. He's still in his long-sleeved white shirt, which has dried just fine despite getting snowed on. His dimple is creased, as if he's been smiling from watching me gape at his kitchen.

I shrug out of his coat, fold it, and set it on the island.

Without the warmth and scent of the wool, I feel exposed. Even more unsure of what to do.

"Are you nervous?"

"No," I lie, tangling my fingers together. "I'm wondering what I'm doing here."

"I told you, I want you safe."

The question hovers on my tongue for a moment before I find my bravery and blurt, "How do I know I'm safe with you?"

"Do you believe in fate?" he asks.

I stare at my fingers. I kinda do, but I don't want to admit it. "No."

"Right. You will." He leaves the door frame and walks further into the kitchen. "Would you like something to drink?"

"Sure."

"An espresso, perhaps?" Now I know he is amused by me.

I roll my eyes at him and he chuckles outright. He opens a cabinet, revealing a space-age-looking espresso machine built right into the wall, like a safe.

"*Un latte*, then. I will steam the milk." He lets his finger dance over the buttons, turning the machine on and programming it with practiced ease. "Trust me."

Trust me. For some reason, I do. Not only with coffee drinks.

The machine does its work, and Royal sets the tiny cup and saucer on the island next to me. But he must see my uncertainty because he comes close, crowding into my space. A Royal invasion, but I don't hate it. I'm too busy drinking in his beauty and his scent.

He puts a finger to my lips. For a moment, he just rubs my bottom lip as if fascinated by its smoothness. I feel his touch all the way down to between my legs.

"Would you feel better if I let you call Mr. Rossi?" he murmurs.

"Yes."

He drops his hand. Without moving out of my space, he pulls out his phone and dials a number. He holds it to my ear, holding my gaze as we both listen to it ring.

"Hello?"

Relief trickles down my spine as I recognize my boss's voice. "Mr. Rossi? It's Leah—are you all right?"

"Ah, Leah. Yes. I'm fine. The doctor is here. He stitched me up. Now he's looking at Cedella."

"The doctor came there?" I repeat, because I've never heard of a doctor doing house calls.

"Yes. He check me first. The men are downstairs, cleaning. It is a miracle."

"Men? What men?"

But Mr. Rossi doesn't seem to hear. "Thank you, Leah," he's gushing, "for delivering the money."

Right, the money. Royal's men must have delivered it. *Thank you,* I mouth to Royal. He lifts his chin.

"I must go now," Mr. Rossi says in a distracted rush. "Everything will be fine. Big storm today. We will close the shop until it passes. Ciao!"

"Ciao," I say, but he's already hung up.

"The doctor came to his house," I say, because I can't quite believe it.

"I told you I'd take care of it."

"What is going on?" My call with Mr. Rossi didn't explain anything.

"Stefanos made a move, but I was ready. What I didn't anticipate was him targeting the bakery. I had men watching before today, but I had called them away. I'm sorry, *principessa.* I failed you."

Men watching? "Stefanos made a move?" I repeat.

"He did. But you don't need to worry about him anymore. He won't bother you or anyone ever again."

I stare into Royal's coffee-black eyes. All the pieces are falling into place, and I know more than I want to. "Why are you telling me this?"

"I won't keep anything from you, Leah. Not if you ask me. Not if you really want to know."

I squint at him. It's like he's answering a question, but one I haven't yet thought to ask.

"This is a lot." I raise a hand between us, but he captures it. His fingers are long and so warm.

"I know, Leah. But you can trust me." He brings my hand to his lips and kisses my palm. A simple gesture, but one of the most intimate things anyone's ever done to me. The softness of his lips, the reverence in his eyes... something is happening here. I feel it again in my stomach, the seismic shift of fate.

I swallow. "What happens now?"

"Now, you are safe. We will wait out the storm."

Whether he means the snow storm outside, or some metaphorical mafia war, I don't know.

I'm in over my head. This is nuts, but I don't want to step away from Royal. Ever.

Do you believe in fate?

He touches my face with just the tips of his fingers, and brushes his lips over mine again. A light, feathery kiss. When he draws back, his eyes are twin pools of darkness.

"*Bella,*" he breathes, and kisses me again. "You taste so sweet."

His touch turns my thoughts upside down. His lips are like a shot of Strega, warming me. I sway on my feet, gasping. *Why would he kiss me? What would he see in me?* I try to turn my head, and his fingers tighten on my chin. "No, open for me." He tilts my head and I let him guide me into a deeper kiss.

My thoughts tumble out of my mind. Who cares why someone as beautiful as this man is kissing little 'ol me? I'm going to enjoy the moment before he changes his mind.

I surge to my tiptoes and kiss him back. My breasts smash against his chest. I'm clumsy but eager, and Royal seems to enjoy it. He steadies me with hands on my hips, then angles his head, guiding the kiss so our mouths slant across each other, allowing his tongue to probe deeper. The move penetrates the very core of me.

When the kiss ends, I'm shaking, and wet. Royal's hair is disheveled—I may have dug my fingers into it in the throes of the kiss, but he's otherwise as put together as usual, while I'm shaky and flushed.

"Wow." My voice is slurred; I sound drunk.

He chuckles and swipes a thumb over my lips. "I want to taste you, princess," he says. "Will you allow me to do that?"

"Yes," I say slowly.

He scoops me up—I love how easily he picks me up—and marches through a vast dining room, into a dark inner room lined with bookshelves and wood paneling, where he sets me down on an overstuffed armchair. Seating himself on the footstool, he draws off my ugly boots.

"Your feet are cold," he tuts. His big hands swallow my foot, massaging, warming. My thoughts roll through a slow lazy loop. I can't believe I'm in a *mansion* with *the most beautiful man I've ever met* and he's giving me a *foot massage*. Is this a dream?

He leans in to kiss me again and I meet his lips eagerly. His tongue sweeps inside my mouth and my pussy clenches. He's taking more than just a taste.

When he breaks the kiss, we're both panting. "You smell like gingerbread," he murmurs. His knuckles brush the swell of my breasts and my back arches, my body begging for more.

"*Mia zia* made them," he continues, softly swirling his knuckles around my nipple. Even through the fabric of my sweater, the light touch makes me ache. "The cookies of my youth. She kept tubs of them on her stairs, and before guests left, she'd put together a tin to take with them. *Biscotti, caramelle...*"

Visions of cookies dance in my head as Royal pushes up my sweater along with my thin cameo shirt. My pink bralette barely holds back my breasts.

"Yes," he breathes. "I need a taste."

I shiver, and he pauses. "Are you cold?"

I shake my head. I'm not cold. Heat crackles under my skin.

He reaches for a remote beside me and points it at the fireplace in the corner. A click of the button, and the gas-fed flames dance over the white stones.

Royal returns to me, pulling off my top layers to bare my bralette. His hands skim along the sides of my breasts. His thumb circles my nipple and tugs the lace edge of my bralette down. He bends his dark head and his hot breath warms my areola. My head falls back. His tongue flicks my nipple, alternating with his finger too. There's a slight pinch as he sets his teeth around my nipple, and tugs. My whole body is rising and falling, riding the waves of sensation.

His hands find my hips and peel down my black leggings. The move pulls me down with it. My back's on the seat chair, my hair spread out in a dark halo around my face. When I look down, Royal is kneeling between my legs. His long, elegant fingers tug but my leggings are stuck.

"Do you like these?" he asks.

I shake my head, trying to lift my bottom to help him. Instead of tugging again, he rips the seam. The fabric tears under his hands and he tosses the shreds away. My yoga pants were cheap, but damn. It's the first time I've seen Royal anything but perfectly controlled.

Now my pussy is within his reach, protected only by a pair of panties with pink cupcakes on them. He studies it like I'm an espresso machine he's about to take apart and put back together. Like he's mapping out the ways to make me purr.

He extends a long finger and traces up and down the seam of my pussy. His touch through my panties makes my toes scrunch.

He hooks his fingers in the sides of my panties. A jerk, and he's ripped them, too.

"I'll buy you more," he promises.

I'm too turned on to protest. I've never had a man look at me like this, staring at my pussy with the intensity of a starving man offered a perfect peach.

He swipes his thumb up and down, collecting juices. Tilting his head in that familiar way of his, he sucks my essence off his thumb. Tremors ripple through my tummy.

My head falls back. A flush is already spreading over my chest. I'm pretty sure I just had a mini orgasm. "What are we doing?" I ask the ceiling.

"I want to taste you. And, *cara mia*, I always get my way." He lowers his dark head between my legs. His fingers stroke the sensitive skin above my knee. He turns his head to kiss the faint, shiny stretch marks I've had on my inner thighs since puberty, when I gained my curves. He seems fascinated by every one. His tongue glides up and down my seam, feeling incredible. Wet and wonderful, it's so much better than my fumbling fingers. It circles my clit and goes back to lapping at my folds.

All too soon, my body clenches in on itself. My knees automatically close, but Royal holds them open so he can keep licking—long, insistent swipes that intensify the tremors until they threaten to rip me apart. My thighs strain under his grip. He's holding me down, and it whips my climax to greater heights. My head thrashes back and forth.

Finally, the white hot edge of my orgasm passes. I relax, letting the aftershocks flow through me.

After a few final swipes of his tongue, Royal raises his head. His face is as darkly beautiful as ever. His lips are wet. He licks them.

"I've never done that," I say. It's true. My ex-boyfriend never did that for me. I never orgasmed with him.

Royal sets his palm on my pussy and grinds down gently. His touch grounds me, even as it sparks new arousal that threatens to send me soaring higher.

"This is the beginning," he says.

CHAPTER 4

oyal

"That was amazing," Leah sighs. She's curled in the chair. My own cock is pressed against my slacks, but I force myself to rise and fetch a warm washcloth from the closest bathroom. I return, and press it against her slick and stimulated pussy, cleaning and soothing all at the same time. I have plans for her pussy, and I want to keep it in good working order.

That's how I see the world. Machines that need to be fixed. Pipes and joints and screws that should be fitted together so things can run smoothly.

From the first moment I saw Leah, I knew she could benefit from my care. She's poor, overworked, tired. No hope, and no way out. I can fix all that.

And she will fix me. She is the last piece I need to be complete.

"Tell me about yourself," I order as I clean her.

She blinks at me, her long black lashes framing innocent eyes. "What do you want to know?"

"Everything."

"Why?"

I stroke her cheek. Is it too early to tell her why? This house is now her home. My bed is the only one she'll sleep in. For the rest of her life, she'll be beside me.

Maybe it's too soon to tell her all this.

"Because I want to know," I say. She'll need to get used to my orders sooner rather than later. She's already most of the way there. "But if you're tired of talking, there are other things we can do. More I can show you."

Her eyes drop to the bulge in my pants. She gulps then licks her lips, and I'm tempted to take her again. To teach her all the things I want her to know. All the pleasure she's yet to explore.

"No," she says slowly, reluctantly. "I'll tell you everything."

"Good." I scoop her up and sit back down in the chair with her in my lap. Her lips part but she doesn't protest. There's a cashmere blanket beside the chair. I shake that out and tuck it around her. She looks incredible, her dark skin glowing in the shadows, her curves framed in soft wool.

I wait a beat, in case she finds her voice. But I can only hold back so long before I tell her, "You're so beautiful."

She blinks at me. The firelight gleams in her dark curls.

"Um, thank you." She ducks her head.

She's uncomfortable with compliments. Something for me to work on.

"I guess I should tell you… I have no family. Well, besides the Rossis."

She bites her lip and I stroke her knee, running a finger over the sliver of skin poking out of the blanket to encourage her to continue. "The couple who owns the *Panetteria*?" I ask.

"Yes. They look after me in their own way."

"Continue."

"My foster family said I could have a job. I was one of several children they took in. It was loud and crowded, and so I got out of the house as much as possible." She hesitates and then says in a rush, as if she wants to get it out quickly, "My father died in an accident when I was little, my mom died of cancer when I turned fifteen."

"I'm sorry, *principessa*." I run a hand over her silky curls. "You've suffered."

"Not that much." She's biting her lip again. I touch her bottom lip the way I did in the kitchen, admiring its smoothness and the way the brown fades to blush pink and back again. She has a little gap between her front teeth. It's absolutely adorable.

"I've had a good life. The Rossis are very kind. They even wanted to take me in, let me live with them once. Only…"

"What is it, pet?"

She squirms in my lap. "Mrs. Rossi is not well, and it's a lot to take care of her. They thought it would be better if I stayed in foster care and stayed in school."

"Is that what you wanted?"

"I want Mrs. Rossi to get better."

Hmm. This is something I might be able to help with. "Do you know her diagnosis?" I make a note to call the doctor later, to confer.

Now there's a little line between her brows. I'd smooth it out like I did her bottom lip, but I don't want to draw attention to her worry. Instead, I wait quietly. It's ecstasy and agony, having her weight in my lap in this quiet, dark room. The firelight plays over her perfect features.

Finally, she says, "She has rheumatoid arthritis. It progressed really fast. When she turned forty-two, she could barely move. She told Mr. Rossi to divorce her but he wouldn't do it." She blows out a breath. "Why am I telling you all of this?"

"Because I asked you. And you wanted to."

She looks around the room as if seeing it for the first time. "You ripped off all my clothes."

I come to my feet, hefting her in my arms. She's all silky brown skin and hair and curves. The perfect armful. "Come." I stride out of the library and up the stairs to my bedroom. I want her to be comfortable, and that means keeping ahead of her nervousness. It's time to show her around her new home.

* * *

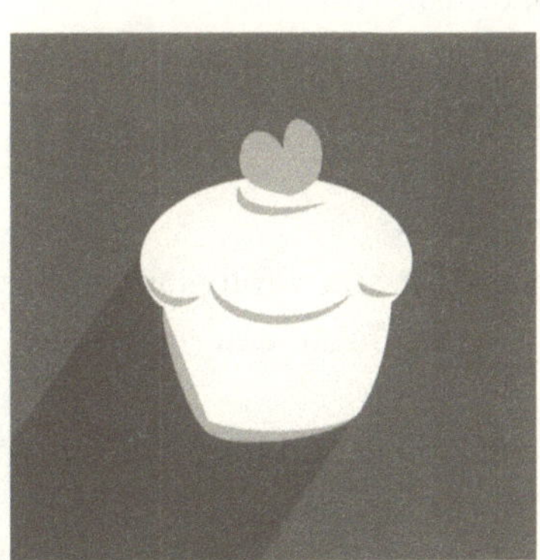

LEAH

ROYAL CARRIES me up a grand staircase. I'm wearing a blanket and a bralette and nothing else. He ripped up the rest of what I was wearing. I'm going to have to deal with that at some point. Later.

I'm still a little floaty. Orgasm endorphins.

Royal climbs the stairs, and we pass a crystal and gold chandelier that's big as a car. "Is it just you who lives here?"

"The staff are off for the day." He carries me down a long hall decorated with gilt-framed paintings that look like they belong in an art museum. When we reach the end, he steps through double doors into a dark bedroom suite that's five times the size of my tiny apartment. "Do you want to wash up? I can draw you a bath." He sets me down but stays close, which is good because I'm unsteady on my feet.

"Or you can just let me go home. If I can charge my phone, I can call a ride."

Royal's eyes narrow. He heads to the window and twitches aside the thick, velvet curtain. The air beyond the glass is a wall of bluish white.

"We're snowed in. My driver is off for the rest of the day, but we should get a plow soon."

"Snowed in?"

"Mmmhmmm."

I narrow my eyes at him. "You planned this."

His cheek curves. "You can teach me how to make *strazzate*."

He lets the curtain fall and his form is draped in darkness once again.

"Here." He takes a limp garment and holds it up. It's a brocade dressing gown, Royal-sized. "You can have a bath later."

Royal already cleaned me up, but I take a moment to myself just so I can explore the massive black marble bathroom. There's a huge steam shower that could hold an orgy. A bathtub made for three—or one long-legged mafioso and a curvy girl like me.

I come out wrapped in his robe, wading through the hem pooling at my feet. I've knotted the sash around my waist, and the front falls into a deep V that showcases my cleavage.

Royal freezes at the sight of me, and it takes the edge off

my nervousness. I have curves for days, and he seems mesmerized by them.

He beckons and when I come to stand in front of him, he kneels and slides my feet into slippers. Unlike the dressing gown, they're the perfect size for my small feet. Probably from another overnight guest. Royal probably has a different woman in his bed every night.

I'm not going to think too hard about that.

There's a side table against the wall full of framed photos. On the end is one of Royal and a stunning, dark-eyed woman. She's tall and thin with olive skin and sleek brown hair. She and Royal are arm in arm, her in a ball gown, him in a tux. A matching set.

My heart sinks. That's who Royal should be with. Someone beautiful and glamorous, like him.

I put my hand on my soft belly, feeling a little sick.

Royal sees the move and misinterprets it. "Are you hungry?"

"A little."

His dark eyes gleam as he draws me close. "I have a craving," he murmurs in my ear, like it's a secret. "For *un biscotto*." A cookie.

I can do cookies. I take a deep breath. "Then let's go to the kitchen."

Once we're in the kitchen, my instincts take over. Royal may be king of his territory and castle, but here, I'm in charge.

"I need flour, sugar, baking powder, salt, eggs, butter or oil." I list off items while Royal stands there with an amused expression on his face. He directs me to the pantry and fetches the items I point to. "Do you have a sifter?"

"I have no idea." He watches patiently as I rummage around the cavernous cabinets in his kitchen. Turns out he has everything I need, from a sifter to two entire sets of Le

Creuset cookware, one in Cerise, one in Chambray. Seven types of cocoa, and three types of almonds—raw, blanched, and in the shell.

I even find a mini blow torch for caramelizing the tops of creme brûlee, along with a double set of custard ramekins. I file this info away for later baking sessions in Royal's house. Which is ridiculous. There will be no later. This is just some crazy one-night stand. Common for a guy as rich and hot as Royal.

After he gets his fill of me, I'll be right back to my little life. I only wish his wasn't so glamorous in comparison to mine. It'll be hard to go back to my usual shabby surroundings, even if that's where I belong.

"Where's my coat?" I ask briskly. Royal must have put it away while I was drooling over the complete set of All-Clad pots and pans. He disappears into a room off the kitchen, and returns with my thin coat.

"Why do you need this?" he asks. His voice is soft, but there's an edge to it. "Are you cold?"

"No." I dig in my pocket and find the torn scrap of paper I tucked there what feels like a lifetime ago. "I'm making this." I lay the recipe flat on the marble island. "I need Strega."

Royal finds a bottle in a liquor cabinet. When he sets it down, there's a look on his face that's close to triumph. He's brought two shot glasses and he fills one to the brim.

He sips a little off the top before putting it to my lips. "Taste." The digestive burns down my throat, leaving an herbal taste in my mouth and a glowing warmth in my stomach.

I sputter a little but find the breath to say, "Good."

He shoots the rest of the glass and dips his head to mine. "Just a little taste," he breathes against my lips. This time, I watch his face as he kisses me. His eyes are closed, long lashes fanning over his dark cheeks. His lips are sipping, pulling on mine, persuading them to open. His tongue touches mine. A little jolt of electricity goes through me.

"It's okay, *principessa*." His thumb strokes my cheek, soothing me. "You're such an innocent, little one."

I wrinkle my nose. "I've got you fooled, then."

He chuckles and leans in for another taste, but I stop him with a firm hand. "Not until I'm done baking."

He could easily overpower me, but he lets me push him back. He leans against a cabinet with his arms folded, and watches me. He's lost his cufflinks but he's still in his dress shirt, his sleeves rolled up to reveal his strong forearms. I'm tempted to put him to work chopping almonds or measuring cocoa but he's so pretty standing there.

"So how long have you lived here?" I ask when I've mostly finished making the batter. All that's left is rolling the cookies into shape.

"My father bought this place some time ago. It's close to our territory."

"So you grew up here?"

"I grew up in the Old Country, raised by my aunt. Italian was my first language. You can tell, by the way I talk."

"Not your accent," I say, dividing the dough in half. It's easier to talk to someone so beautiful when my hands are occupied with my favorite thing. "But yes, from the way you sometimes construct your sentences. And, of course, you speak Italian."

"You recognize the language?"

"Mr. Rossi says things in Italian all the time."

Royal reaches for a newly shaped cookie and I swat his hand. "There's raw egg in the dough."

A smile plays over his lips but he allows me to fend him off. He does move around the island to stand directly behind me. I'm short and petite enough he can rest his arms on the counter on either side of me. Neither his fine black slacks or the voluminous dressing robe I'm wearing disguise the hard probe of his cock.

Is that a rolling pin in your pocket? I'm half tempted to ask, but I keep making cookies. I've made another six *strazzate* when a light finger comes to play with one of the curls at the nape of my neck. I ignore it, and the way his cock is firmly pressed against my bottom. It's almost a game.

"So your father lives here?" I ask.

"No. Not anymore. No one but me." Royal keeps toying with my hair. It feels like he's smoothing out a curl, and letting it spring back into place.

I want to ask more, but his touch is making my hands shake. Under the robe, my bare pussy is dripping. I squeeze my thighs together, but it doesn't help.

The last row of cookies is turning out to be kind of a mess.

"My father didn't approve of me," Royal says out of nowhere.

"Why not?"

"He thought I was weak. Unworthy. He didn't understand the way my mind worked. But *mia zia* saw something in me."

I'm done making the rows of *strazzate*. I dip my fingers in a warm bowl of water, rinsing them.

Royal's warm breath puffs against my nape. "Turns out my father was wrong, and she was right. I'm very close to fulfilling my destiny. I see the pieces of the puzzle, laid out before me." He splays his hands on the counter as if showing me a picture in the sugar-dusted marble. "That's how my mind works. The puzzle is almost complete. I just need one more piece."

Royal's trying to tell me something and I don't know what. I turn, still in the circle of his arms. I'm trapped between the island and his taut frame. "Royal, I don't know what's going on here."

He tilts his head in that assessing way of his. His hair falls into his face, but otherwise he might as well be a statue, carved from marble by a master sculptor. "My aunt was something of a witch. *Una Bennedetta.* Do you know it?"

I shake my head.

"She's gifted a little, in the Sight. The gift of prophecy. She said, 'When you meet a woman who makes *le strazzate di matera* like I do, you must take her and marry her.' You understand?"

Do I understand? The words—sure, I understand. But what he's telling me? Not a clue. "No," I whisper.

"Don't worry. You will." He tugs the lapel of his robe down my shoulder. "You're covered in sugar again."

He dips his head and closes his mouth over my smooth skin, under the pretense of lapping up the sugar. My head falls back, allowing him full access. His tongue seems to have a direct line to my pussy, no matter where it touches. He licks and sucks his way up to my neck, holding me still with his hand around my throat. I've never had a guy take charge of me like Royal. I've also never had a guy so confident in the ins and outs of my body. My ex barely cared if I got off. Royal seems to have made it his mission in life.

My eyes are half closed by the time he raises his head.

"Sweet," he murmurs.

I rise to my tiptoes, drawing his shoulders down so I can kiss him, tasting the powdered sugar on his lips. "So are you."

"Not really. But you are sweet enough for the both of us." His large hand comes to palm my breast. The lights flicker. For a second, I think it's a trick of my mind, another eclectic shock from Royal's touch, but when I blink, the lights are still off. So's the oven.

There's a hum like a room of engines turning on, and the lights switch back on.

"The generators kicked in," Royal says. "Up here, a tree

falls on the lines during a deep freeze. We have power to last months."

This house is so extra. A generator and two sets of Le Creuset? I could stay here forever.

Night has darkened the kitchen window. I can barely see beyond a few feet. "Still snowing," I say.

"Yes, it's quite a blizzard. We might be stuck inside for several days."

"What about the Rossis? Do you think they'll be okay?"

"I have men watching the shop. They'll look after the Rossis. I'll have them deliver food, water. A generator to make sure they have power."

"Why do you have men watching the shop?"

"Protection. In case Stefanos' remaining men make a move. It's unlikely, but I'm taking no chances."

I ponder this. "The men who helped clean up the broken glass. They're ones you sent?"

He nods.

"Why are you doing this? Helping us, I mean." It makes sense that he'd want to expand his territory, but all this work to protect a small bakery? Seems like a lot for the purpose of a one-night stand. But... what else could this be?

"I told you I'd fix it." He shrugs with his hands in his pockets. "I'm fixing it. That's what I do. I want to help you."

"Why?"

"It's too soon to tell you that." His beautiful mouth curves. "How about I show you instead?"

And that's how I find myself on my back on the grand dining room table. Royal sits in the fancy chair at the head of the table, looking like the lord of his realm. He's still fully clothed, while I'm in nothing but his robe and my last remaining item of clothing—a flimsy bralette.

He pulls apart the robe I'm wearing. I get the feeling he likes seeing me in his clothes. He plays with my bralette, tugging it down under my breasts. His thumb hits my nipple and sensation detonates between my legs.

"We should watch the cookies," I say softly, even though I don't really care.

"You set a timer," he mutters. With his thumbs, he spreads apart my pussy, staring boldly at it. "Let's see how many times you can come before they're done."

That sounds like a great game.

It's a little weird to be lying on my back on a dining room table, like I'm a meal to be eaten, but when Royal finishes kissing his way up my inner thighs, he gets down to eating my pussy. Feasting, really. Long swipes of his tongue intersperse with hungry nibbles on my pouty lower lips.

I come within a minute, but he doesn't stop.

"Royal." I squirm.

"Again." He presses my legs apart. A jolt goes through me as he holds me down.

"Tell me when you're close," he orders.

"I'm close," I gasp almost immediately. "I need—"

He raises his head. His tongue leaves my clit and as soon as the pressure is gone, my building climax ebbs away. My whole pussy pulses.

"No," I whine.

He was working me up, the bastard.

"I thought you were going to see how many times I can come."

"I've decided on a new game."

I reach for him, and he pushes me back down. His fingers go back to brushing my sensitive spots, so I subside against the polished surface of the dining table.

He plays with my pussy and massages the sensitive area around my rear pucker. I lift my head again when his finger probes too close.

"What are you doing?" I clench my bottom. My anal ring tightens. Royal keeps studying and rubbing my bottom hole.

"How does this feel?" he asks, like a doctor testing reflexes.

It feels amazing. Too amazing, for such a naughty spot. Heat floods my face.

"I'm going to test something," he murmurs. I'm about to grab his head and shove him away when he bows and puts his whole mouth over my labia. His tongue thrusts into my sopping entrance. At the same time, he twists and dips his finger inside my ass. My orgasm rips through me. I plant my feet and shake. A few more licks and he's rearing up over me, ripping open his pants and exposing his huge, gorgeous cock. His hands tug my hips down to meet his. He rubs my slick center over his long length before spearing me.

I arch back, my body bowing on the table. Royal's hand comes down on my breast, and for once, it's rough. He squeezes my breast hard as his cock hits the perfect spot. My orgasm begins again.

Royal's arms are planted on the table, his thrusts pushing me up the polished surface. His hair's fallen in his face, his teeth are bared. He's more ferocious and out of control than I've ever seen him.

At the last, he pulls out of my sopping pussy and grips my hips to hold me close.

His cum spurts onto my soft stomach. I gasp, my body jack-knifing with my final climax. Royal leans over me, holding my gaze as I tremble with aftershocks. His fingers come to my face, tracing my nose, my brows, my cheeks and, finally, rubbing my lower lip. I open my mouth and bite down on his thumb, gently. A shudder runs through him.

He pulls me into his lap. I sprawl against his chest as he dips his fingers in his cum, scooping it up and feeding it to me. I suck the salty fluid from his fingers.

"Good girl," he murmurs, and I press my legs together, ready to orgasm again.

My head is swirling in the clouds. There's a buzzing in the background—a long, low sound like an annoyed hornet. The oven timer.

I jolt. "The cookies!"

Royal closes his arms around me, his chest jerking with laughter.

I smack his arm. "How long has the timer been going off?"

"A while." He holds me close when I would scramble off. "Relax. After you set the timer, I programmed the oven to turn off."

"They still might be burned. I need to check them."

"Later," he growls, scooping me into his arms. "I'm not finished with you."

CHAPTER 5

Royal carries me up the stairs, back to the bedroom where he sets me on the bed. "Stay."

I follow orders like a good girl, waiting while he disappears into the bathroom. I scoop my boobs back into my bralette and straighten the straps. My soft belly is sticky with Royal's cum. I feel small in this magnificent room, a disheveled doll set in a richly appointed photoshoot spread in a high-end home living magazine.

Royal returns, and his brows knot together at the sight of me. In the aftermath of the orgasms, I'm wobbly, but I slide to my feet, fidgeting with the robe he gave me.

"What?" I ask, bracing myself for him to tell me he's changed his mind and, snow or not, he's ready for me to go.

"Come." He proffers his hand. My foot catches on the fold of the oversized robe and I stumble. Royal's there to catch me with a frown.

"*Spiacente,*" he apologizes. "I should dress you in a proper sized robe."

"It's okay. I kind of like it."

We step inside the bathroom, and my eyes widen. In the

darkness, candles glow, each one lit, tapers after tapers along the edge of a bathtub filled near to the brim with steaming water. The air is warm with the humidity the bath is giving off, and from the overabundance of glowing candles.

"What is this?" I breathe.

"A bath. I made you dirty, *principessa*. Now I'll make you clean."

He pulls me to the center of the room and then stops, turning to me. He unbuttons his long-sleeved shirt and pulls it off, leaving him in black slacks and an undershirt that bares his biceps. His muscles are hard and sleek, totally droolworthy.

He tosses his dress shirt to the marble floor and I make a little noise.

"You shouldn't throw your clothes aside. They're expensive."

"Mmm," he hums, turning to me with hunger in his dark eyes. He looks like he wants to devour me alive. My face heats up, the steam curling off the water making my skin flushed and warm.

He tugs the robe down my arms and lets it pool at my feet. He fingers the lace of my bralette like he wants to rip it off.

"Don't," I warn. "I like this bralette."

"I'll buy you a new one."

"You already owe me leggings," I scold, and choke on my words when he strips off his undershirt, presenting me with a mouthwatering display of sleek, tan muscles. His skin is a few shades lighter than mine, an olive brown that speaks to his Mediterranean heritage. I tighten my hands to fists before I run my hands all over him. "Never mind," I say. "You don't owe me anything."

"No?" He angles his body, posing a little. Teasing me.

"No." I drag my eyes away from him. "You've already helped a ton. You don't need to buy me anything."

"What if I want to buy you things?"

My reflection in the steamed up mirror has a furrowed brow. *That does not compute.* "Why would you want to do that?"

"I like buying pretty things." He turns me back to him. I'm face to face with the groove between his smooth pecs. My thoughts stutter into nothing.

He thumbs along the lines of my breasts, fingering the lace.

"I like to own them."

He strips me of my last item of clothing, and I let him, holding my arms up obediently.

He bends over me, brushing his lips over the shell of my ear. "I would spend tens of thousands to dress you, just so I could rip those threads from your body." Those whispered words race across my skin, lighting me up from the inside out. My legs are about to give out when his arms close around me. He positions me in front of him, facing the mirror. I let him move me around like I'm a doll, leaning back into his hard body as he lets his hands roam over me. He's still in his slacks, but the expensive fabric does nothing to hide the steel rod of his cock pressing into my bare backside.

Royal's breath warms my neck as he smooths his hands over my hips and soft belly. He cups my breasts and strokes the sensitive sides of my breasts with his thumbs. My curves fill his big palms, a generous handful spilling out of his hold.

He kisses up my neck while I stare at our reflection.

"What are you thinking?" he murmurs.

"I'm curvy," I say.

"You're beautiful." His hand comes to my throat, wrapping around it and turning my head for his kiss. "Open for me, Leah."

And I do. I'll let him do anything he wants to me. If we only have one night together, I'm going to soak up everything I can.

It'll be over all too soon.

* * *

LEAH

I AWAKEN IN DARKNESS, blinking in the blissful warmth. There's a long, hard body pressed up against me. *Royal.* I'm in his bed. Across the dark room, beyond the window panes, snow falls silently.

Last night, Royal gave me a bath. At my request, he kept my hair dry, but personally washed me, running a washcloth over all my curves. I may have had another mini orgasm or two, just from his thorough washing of my princess parts.

He scooped me from the tub, drying me off with the same

thoroughness and intensity he does everything—from fixing espresso machines to giving me orgasms. Then he took me to bed and made it clear how beautiful he thinks I am.

Now I'm in his bed, still drowsy. I twitch in preparation to inch away, and Royal's arm tightens.

"Leah," he murmurs against the back of my neck.

"I wasn't trying to wake you," I whisper. "I should go." A one-night stand only lasts one night. I have no cause to feel disappointed.

"It's snowing. You sleep now." His voice is muffled by my hair.

"What time is it?"

With a soft snarl, he moves, craning around to check the clock. "Six in the morning. February fourteenth."

No wonder I woke up. This is prime baking time.

I push against Royal's hard arm, but it doesn't budge. "I need to get to work."

"The shop is still closed," he says, sounding fully awake now. "Not only because of snow. Your boss is also going to wait until the shop has undergone repairs."

"You talked to him?" After the final round of sexy times, I passed out. Probably only a handful of hours ago.

"My men did."

"He's all right? And Cedella?"

"Both doing fine. We can call them whenever you like."

I lick my lips. Sooner or later, I'm going to need to return home. But maybe I can keep the fantasy a little while longer.

"It's Valentine's Day," I say, even as I let myself relax against Royal.

He nuzzles the back of my neck. "Did you have plans?"

"Not really." I'd be making vanilla cupcakes with strawberry pink frosting, and red velvet cupcakes topped with thick cream cheese frosting.

"No date?"

"Not since my ex dumped me a year ago. The day before Valentine's Day." So he could take the girl he really wanted out on a date. "Since then, I've been alone."

"Not anymore." Royal kisses the back of my neck, his lips soft and sweet. It feels so good, I close my eyes.

"Eventually, I have to go back to my life," I manage in a shaky voice.

"Or... You could stay here with me." He rolls me onto my back and rises over me, a satisfied look on his face. "I have lots to offer... Everything you desire. Stay until I show you it all."

I'm naked and so is he. It's very distracting. "This is ridiculous." My voice comes out a pant.

He's wide awake now. He pushes my legs apart. "You can't leave. We're snowed in." His cock bobs as he looks down at me. "Looks like you'll be here a little while longer."

"I guess." I lick my lips, staring at the dark shape of his cock.

"Come here," he demands, pulling me up with him. I don't even have time to protest before he bundles me into his lap. I look up at him and he kisses me, mouth traveling down my jaw, to my neck. He drags his teeth over my skin, holding me close. It's just the two of us, a sea of blankets, with the snow falling thick and heavy outside.

He tips me back, cradling me in strong arms. My nerves tingle and I tilt my head back, letting him kiss down the line of my shoulder to my breasts. He shifts, laying me down so he can devour my skin, licking over my left breast, pulling my nipple into a tight bud.

"Wait, stop," I say as his hand skims down between my thighs. He pauses and his gaze travels up my body, his eyes intense as he looks at me.

"What is it?"

My cheeks are flushing as I say it, but the words spill out of me. "I want to watch you make yourself feel good," I say.

He makes an amused noise. "*Si?*" He adjusts me in his lap. "Is that what you want?"

I nod and slide off of him, slipping back into the pillows, propping myself up. He presents me with his palm.

"Lick," he commands, and I do. I lap at his hand, painting his skin with my saliva. "Good girl." He takes his cock in hand. It's rock-hard and waiting, the tip flushed as red as my cheeks.

"After this, we do what I want," he says, "since I'm giving you a show."

My mouth goes dry and I nod. Anything, to see him touch himself, show me exactly how he likes it.

"Do you know how long I've thought of this?" he asks me as he grips his rod, his face turning dark. His eyes burn over my skin, and I don't want to ask him how long, or why, because I'm too busy drinking in the look of him, spine steel-straight, head slightly bowed, as he works his hand up and down his length.

My lips part as he watches me watching him. This is the most erotic thing I've ever done in my life. The wet sound of his hand over his skin makes my sex throb. My thighs tighten together.

I want him, that, inside of me.

I feel hot all over, and he groans, spreading his knees, bracing a hand next to me on the sheets as he works himself over.

"After this, you're gonna give me what I want." His words are breathy and thick. His eyes close tight and his hand stills on his cock, his hips hitching like he wants to fuck into his fist. "Lie back, beautiful."

I obey, flattening myself. He straddles me, his heavy

thighs bracing on either side of my body. His cock bobs in front of my face and my mouth opens automatically.

"Is this what you want?" His voice is a soft rasp. "I just bathed you last night. Made you clean. And now you want to be dirty again?"

I'm too overcome to do more than whimper. My breasts are heaving.

He's stroking himself faster now, tipping back his head, caught in his own passion. "Leah," he breathes, and comes. The blast of seed spills from the head of his cock over my lush breasts, frosting my skin with silver.

He leans down, swipes his finger across my coated breasts, and feeds his cum to me. I round my lips and suck hard, pulling on his digit. His gaze goes black.

"*Principessa mia*." He breathes the words like they're a prayer, and bends over to open a drawer, pulling out two black, silk lengths of fabric. He gives me a look that should strike fear right into my heart. But it doesn't.

"Now," he says. "We do what I want."

I hold my breath as he takes my ankles and ties them apart. Then he settles between my bound legs, and licks me until I beg him to stop.

* * *

LEAH

THE SHEETS RUSTLE as I wake up, melting from the dark back into consciousness. My fingers slip along the crisp linen, seeking the warmth I'm starting to get used to finding—

Nothing. My hand closes on empty space and I sit up, my curls tumbling away from my face.

Royal's gone, and my heart squeezes hot and tight in my chest. Light is sliding through the room, gray and overcast. I guess the storm is still haunting us, keeping me here.

The clock on the bedside table has its hour hand pointed to two, and I squeak. *Two in the afternoon?* I haven't slept this late in years.

I need to get up.

The carpet is plush against my feet as I get out of bed, and for a moment I want to leave the blankets rumpled in memorial to an epic night and early morning, but I can't. I smooth the duvet, and straighten the pillows. It seems like a crime to leave things a mess when this bedroom is more beautiful than anything I've seen on HGTV or pinned on my Pinterest board.

Warmth radiates up from the floor, caressing my skin, and I'm very aware that I'm not wearing anything. Me, naked, my curves bare in this beautiful, minimalist shrine to masculinity. Anyone could walk in right now. I sneak across the room, feeling like an intruder in this place, Royal's home.

I squint at the closet doors, wondering if there's something behind them that would work for me. Even a shirt of Royal's would fall down past my thighs. That would be okay to tide me over. It's going to be awkward to figure out what to wear home. *Um, Royal, can you buy me some clothes so I can ride the bus?*

Talk about a walk of shame.

I wrap my hands around the dark onyx door handles, and pull them open.

Lights flare to life in front of me. What I thought was a simple closet is nearly fifteen feet deep and ten across. That's not even the real surprise.

My lips part in shock, and my breath falters to a stop in my throat. This closet doesn't hold a single shred of men's clothing.

Racks line one side, with dresses hung carefully on white velvet hangers. Gentle pink tulle, cream silks, gem-stone velvets, all organized neatly in length and a rainbow of colors. I step in and lift one hand, fingers shaking as I carefully flip a tag that's pinned to a spaghetti strap.

Oscar De La Renta, it reads, and I drop it like it's hot. I reach for the next dress, and can't contain my gasp. *Dolce & Gabbana.* I flick through labels. *The Row, Valentino, Zimmerman*—

The blood is rushing to my head as I turn. The opposite wall is lined with neat shelves, rows of softly folded sweaters in what has to be cashmere in glowing colors, waiting to be slipped on and worn.

Whose closet is this? The picture of the beautiful woman with Royal flashes through my head. Is this her stuff?

The closet door swings shut behind me with a whisper. I whirl, and freeze. Hanging on the back of the door is a huge white monstrosity of tulle and satin. A wedding dress.

What the fuck?

I'm going to vomit all over the plush carpeting. Royal has a fiancée, and she has the nicest closet I've ever seen. Tens of thousands of dollars' worth of never worn clothing, complete with tags.

Hang on. Take a breath. There's a lot of wonderful things Royal has said to me.

There's a lot he's not telling you, too.

I've got to get out of here.

I need something to wear. In a daze, I hold a shirt up to my bare chest. It's my size. Plus sized. Not made to fit a tall, thin Italian Barbie, but a short, curvy girl like me.

My mouth is full of ash. Royal's girlfriend… fiancée… is my size. *Guess he has a type.*

I reach for a drawer and pull it open, hoping to find something normal, like Target underwear, and instead there's a pile of frothy lace, and what I swear is a tag reading *Agent Provocateur.* Once again, in my size.

My heart-rate is through the ceiling. All those things he said, all the nice things he made me feel… Lies.

Rifling through drawers, I find a bra and underwear that looks normal-ish and not worth a few hundred dollars, and quickly pull on a plain sweater, and jeans. The denim is soft against my fingers, the cut flaring on my curves. When I turn, I catch sight of myself in a floor-length mirror edged with frosting-pink metal flowers blooming along the gilt frame.

Everything fits perfectly. It only twists the knife in further.

This isn't a fairytale. Royal isn't a handsome prince. Even if he did single-handedly double the amount of orgasms I've had in my lifetime—all in one night.

I reach for a pair of winter boots, black leather and exactly my size, and keep them in my hand as I sneak out of the closet and cozy up to the bedroom door. It's cracked open, and when I peek outside, there's no one there. Relief floods me. Getting out of here is the right thing to do. There's a reason Royal wasn't with me when I woke up. This was a one-night stand, and it's time for it to end.

I pad down the hall in socked feet, keeping on the thick carpet so the flooring doesn't creak. I need to get to the kitchen, get my coat. Call a ride—if I can find a charger for my phone. Maybe Royal will be out, and I can do my walk of shame without an audience.

We had a magical night, and now it's over. What did I expect? I never had any luck with men, especially not on Valentine's Day.

I'm halfway down the stairs, clutching my boobs so they don't bounce in this new bra, when I hear low, murmuring voices floating toward me. I hold my breath and creep down the final steps.

A door to my left is pushed open a few inches, and I press myself into the wall, watching the two people inside a book-shelf-lined study.

Royal. And another guy who looks a lot like him. One of the many cousins.

I should keep to the plan and continue sneaking out, but a glimpse of Royal's beautiful face in profile roots my feet to the rug.

Royal. His face embodies the word, regal and perfect. Just the sight of him makes heat roll through me as I remember all the things he's done to me. All the things he's made me feel. Oh god, I feel like I'm going to throw up again.

"Spit it out, Enzo," Royal commands, and I jump.

The man who must be Enzo stops fiddling with a marble paperweight and puts it back on the desk.

"I know what you're planning," Enzo says. "*La Famiglia* requires you to be married to inherit the throne. Is it really going to be her?"

Those words fall to the floor like billiard balls, heavy and hard, and they stop my heart right in its tracks. A cold flush, descending from my head on down my body, has me nearly shivering. I grit my teeth to keep them from clacking.

So it's true. The small part of me that was hoping he was only storing the wedding dress in his bedroom for a friend, dies. He really does have a fiancée.

Royal sighs, and turns away from Enzo, staring into a crackling fireplace.

"There is no one else," he says. "I can have nobody else." He leans on the mantel. There sits another collection of photos in intricate, polished silver frames. His gaze lingers on one in particular, and my heart stutters its way through a series of painful beats.

Of course. The beautiful woman in the photo. Who else would belong at Royal's side?

A sour taste blooms on my tongue. I'm an idiot. A plaything. Something to keep him occupied while he brooded over his impending marriage to Sophia Loren.

And the way he said it. *I can have nobody else.* He doesn't want anyone but her.

Time for me to go. I tiptoe down the hall to find the kitchen, and the side room with my coat. Forget charging my phone and calling a ride. I've got to get out of here before Royal finds me.

I push my feet into the boots and open the door. The wind lashes me across the face, tugging at my curls and promising a frosty walk. Maybe I can get to a bus stop before I freeze to death. But nothing will warm the frozen place inside of me, the iced-over blood sluggish in my veins.

Tears bite at my lashes, welling up in my eyes. The snow crackles under my feet, the top layer frosty-frozen, and the underneath powdery and slippery.

The driveway hasn't been plowed since the snowfall, but I shove my hands in my pockets. I'll make it out of here on my own two feet, with the battered and tattered threads of my pride wrapped around me like a cape. I'm *not* his plaything. And he can't toy with me, not anymore.

I stride forward and, not twenty feet out, my foot hits something under the snow. I go down flailing, face-planting in the cold fluff. Snow stings my eyes, and frosts my hair. I lie there for a moment, wishing I was anywhere else. Nobody in the history of the world has ever been as pathetic as I am.

"*Principessa?*" That smoothed over, melted-chocolate voice finds me, and before I can roll on my side to give him a wavering middle-finger, Royal's arms are around me.

He picks me up, pulling me out of the snow like I weigh as little as a snowball. I'm too soggy and cold to protest. Much.

"What d-do you th-think you're d-doing?" I try to sound snippy, but my teeth are chattering.

"What did I tell you about that coat?" he murmurs back. He curls me to his chest and despite myself, I melt into him. "I see you found some clothes. You look good," he gives a soft *tsk*, "but it's too cold for you to be out like this."

He strides back the way I came, the snow crunching under his shoes.

My hands ball up into fists, but they lie uselessly in my lap, his arms pinning mine against me so I can't do anything but be carried, like a helpless kitten.

"I'm n-not g-going b-back," I say.

"No?" Royal's chest rumbles with an amused growl, and he carries me up the steps and back into the house. He sets me down in the grand entrance and closes the door. I feel about two feet tall.

"What were you thinking, going out with so few layers on?" He fusses over me, stripping the coat from me despite my struggles. "You could catch a chill. I should turn you over my knee." He takes my hands between his and rubs them, like he did in the SUV. The memory smacks me so hard, I can't catch my breath. "If you wanted to go for a walk with me, you only had to ask."

"I wasn't—I was running away, from you, you and your fiancée," I spit out.

Royal cocks an eyebrow at my words.

"Fiancée?" he repeats, like he doesn't know what I'm talking about.

"I heard you talking to Enzo. He said you needed to marry."

"Ah, yes." Royal straightens, looking down at me from his regal height.

"And I found a closet full of clothes—" I reach for my anger and it's right there. I point a finger at his chest. "Right there in your bedroom. Women's clothes. *Her* clothes. I can't believe you would—"

"Did they fit you?" he interrupts.

"What?" I falter, my finger wilting.

"Did the clothes fit? I specified your size."

I open my mouth but nothing comes out.

"Leah, the clothes are for you." His expression darkens. "Did you think I had them here for another woman?"

"Yes?" The image of the wedding dress blooms big and white in my head. Was it also in my size?

"Oh, *principessa.*" He lifts his hand and I flinch, but he simply brushes a gentle finger over my cheek. "You have much to learn."

I swallow several times to find my voice. "For me?" I squeak. All those dresses, the lingerie. "You got them for me?"

"I told you I'd replace what I ripped off you."

He did say that. "I thought you'd get me a gift card."

That indulgent smile is back on his face. He shakes his head slightly.

My brain is short-circuiting. "But that's tens of thousands of dollars' worth of clothes—"

"Nothing less than you deserve." He grips my chin with light fingers and dips his head to my ear. "Shall we have a little fashion show later? You dress up for me. I'll kiss you and tell you how beautiful you look in the clothes I bought you. And then I'll rip them off."

A high-pitched whimper escapes me before I can gulp it back. Royal raises his head, laughing at the expression on my face. *I would spend tens of thousands to dress you,* he told me last night. Was it only last night?

There are too many thoughts swimming in my head. "I don't understand."

"I see I have more explaining to do." The humor leaves his face like it never existed. "You were a busy little baker this morning. Cooking up the wrong ideas. Eavesdropping." He traces the line of my jaw. He's crooning but there's a dangerous glint to his eyes. "I'm going to need to break you of that habit. In my world, it's not safe to listen to the wrong conversations."

I can only stare up at him.

"It's all right. I'll keep you safe. But let me make one thing clear." He dips his head. "I will marry…" His eyes bore into mine, demanding I pay attention to every word he says. "You. You will be my bride."

"Wh-what?" My lips part, but no more words come out. He smoothes a thumb over my lower lip, teasing me. My insides quiver and it has nothing to do with the winter air swirling around us.

"I'll give you everything, *principessa,* everything you want. You will be faithful to me, and bear my children. Is that not what you thought would happen?" He leans down and kisses the shock right out of me, the flare of heat from his lips chasing away the cold. His mouth is heated and heavy on mine. He traces the path his thumb made with his tongue.

I crush myself against his hard chest. My mainframe is crashing and nothing makes sense, but it doesn't matter when Royal kisses me.

I'm up on my tiptoes, asking for more, when he pulls

away. His eyes are dark, shadowed, his mouth pulling into a thin and serious line.

"But first," he draws out the words, and my heartstrings along with it, "you need to learn a lesson. My wife will be loyal and faithful, always. Do you understand?"

I blink at him.

"Loyalty means not running. Faithfulness means asking questions and not assuming. There will be punishment for you leaving like that."

"Punishment?"

"Yes. You could have been hurt." He bends down and scoops me into his arms. "When I'm done with you, you will not run again."

Royal carries me to the dark bedroom and sets me down on the bed. He looks me over, like he's checking me for damage, and his lips press together in a thin, unimpressed line. My stomach dips and swoops, hating that I've let him down.

"This looks lovely on you," he comments, fingering the sleeve of my sweater. "Now that you know it is yours, do you like your surprise?" His eyes track over to the closet doors.

"You can't buy me with fancy clothes," I mumble, even though part of me wants to swoon in his arms.

I like to buy pretty things, he told me. *I like to own them.*

Royal tugs off my sweater and boots while I wrestle with my feelings. I could let myself go last night, telling myself it was one night. But now?

"Royal, please." I catch his shoulders as he's unbuttoning my jeans. "This is crazy. We just met. You can't buy me all those things." I can't even discuss the 'you will be my bride' part. It's too nuts.

"No?" He's back to being amused. He finishes pulling off my wet jeans and rubs his warm hands up my freezing legs, which, frankly, is a relief. Once again, I'm cocooned in Royal's dark room and delicious scent, ready to succumb to his demands.

But I can't let go like I did last night. It will mean too much to me. These feelings growing in my chest—they over-whelm me. They make me want to run.

He seems to sense the shift in my emotions, and shakes his head. "You will not," he says, pressing me back to the bed. "I will not allow it."

"What?"

"You think I do not know you, inside and out?" He strokes back my tangle of curls, spreading my hair across the pillow. "You will not run again. I will never do anything less than treasure you, *principessa*. But first..." his voice is deep and smoky, whispering over my skin, "there is punishment for you, for trying to run." He kisses the tender lobe of my ear, licking over it in a way that has me grabbing for the front of his shirt to pull him close.

He rears out of reach. "Lie back."

He waits until I obey, and turns to the bedside table to rummage in a drawer. At the sight of the ties in his hands, my mouth goes dry. My body remembers how he tied me down last night, and is making ready for him. Adrenaline fizzes in my bloodstream. My heartbeat is wild in my chest.

"Give me your wrists." He's got four silk strips of fabric. Two for my wrists, and two for my ankles. He ties me down the way he wishes, and pulls the bra I'm wearing down so the whole thing props up my breasts. I'm still in the plain panties. If he rips these ones off, at least he paid for them.

He paid for a whole closet full of them. I can't think about that.

Royal rises over me, studying me like a king observing his chattel. He skims a finger over my soft belly and cups his hand between my legs. His palm presses into my pussy. "This belongs to me."

Oh. My. God.

"Say it." His eyes are demon dark. He drags his hand over my sex, rubbing lightly. "Tell me, Leah, who this belongs to."

"You?" My voice is a barely a huff.

"Me." A wicked grin tilts his lips. He keeps rubbing me.

"Royal—"

"Shhh, little one. No more talking. Just feel."

My thighs are shaking. His touch is light, too light for me to come. I squirm, wanting more stimulation.

"Be still," he orders, releasing me. I whimper, wanting his touch back.

He leaves me, going to stand in the shadows by the bed. He's fiddling with something on his sleeves—his cufflinks. They clink as he sets them down on the bedside table.

He rolls up his sleeves, his gaze never leaving mine. By the time he's bared his forearms, my chest is heaving like I've run up a flight of stairs.

"Such a good girl," he murmurs. "So obedient."

I don't know why those words thrill me.

"You look so lovely, bound and waiting. I could eat you up."

Oh please, yes.

"But first, you need to be punished for trying to run." He heads to the foot of the bed and settles between my splayed legs. He kisses my shaking knees, clamping his hands on each one to hold me down. I couldn't escape, even if I wanted to. Royal's dark hair tickles the inside of my thighs as he licks up one and then the other, teasing the sensitive flesh. His tongue finds each of my stretch marks and traces them. A lick, a kiss, nothing but worship. My pussy throbs, ready for his mouth.

Hot breath hits the gusset of my panties. "You're not to come, not until I tell you," he says, and before I can even ask a question, or protest, his tongue is on me, licking over the panties. The thin fabric lets me feel everything, while dampening the sensation enough to keep me from coming. I arch my back, pushing myself into his mouth. I grab the ties securing me to the bed, hanging on as waves of ecstasy swamp me, stealing my breath. Royal runs his hands up my thighs, holding me open to him, holding me still for the lashing of his tongue. He's pressing me forward, pushing me toward the edge.

Then he raises his head.

"No!" I was so close. I shut my eyes tight and bury the whine that wants to crawl up the back of my throat. I know he'll show me no mercy, even if I complain.

This is my punishment.

I have to take it.

"Are you going to run away again?" His voice is a soft rumble that rolls right through me. I bite my lip.

"You're not letting me come." I can't help how petulant I sound, and he chuckles.

"No. You don't come until I say so. You don't run unless I tell you to. You *belong* here, to me. It's fate." He hooks the gusset to the side and lowers his mouth to my core again. My whole body lights up. No one manipulates my body this well. Not me. Not my ex. Only Royal.

My pleasure is spiraling out of control. My inner muscles clench on air, on nothing. *I'm so close.*

Right before I go over, he lifts his head, looking up at me from between my trembling thighs.

"Do not," he warns me, and I swallow hard, trying to stop myself from tipping over the edge.

"Please," I beg softly, trying to put all my apology in my voice for running, for even thinking that I could escape him.

He strokes the insides of my thighs, craning his neck to kiss the stretch marks on my soft belly. "You have much to learn, *cara mia.* And I am going to teach you." Now he's risen up to nuzzle at my breasts. "You are going to be my good girl. My wife. All this," he palms my pussy, "belongs to me."

My breath hitches. My eyes flutter.

"Look at me, Leah."

I open my eyes wide, meeting his dark gaze.

"I will never allow you to doubt how beautiful you are. I will spend the rest of my life, every last waking hour, making sure you know that you are a gift to the world."

His palm rocks against my folds, gently rubbing. Destroying all thought.

"You are perfect. And you are mine."

I strain my bonds. I need more.

But he takes his hand away. He stands, his fingers going to the buttons of his shirt. I whimper as the white linen and sleek undershirt fall to the ground. His bare chest is muscled and magnificent. He thumbs open his trousers. His pants and boxer briefs hit the floor. I get a few precious seconds to ogle his perfect body before he's climbing onto the bed, sliding between my legs to drape his heavy form over me.

He kisses me, intense and insistent, tongue demanding access, the faint, earthy taste of myself on his lips. The flavor has my cheeks heated and blushing. His cock is in his hand. He guides it to my sopping center, spreading me open with the head. He drives inside me, and I cry out. His expression is serene as he fucks me hard into the sheets, like he knew this is where'd we be, right now, down to the minute and second.

Like he knew I'd try to run.

And that he'd catch me.

"You think you can run from me? You think I'd just let you go? That's not the type of man I am." He slams his hips into mine, filling me to the brim. "I'm the man who takes what he wants." He grinds against me. "And I want to own you."

Oh. My. God.

"You're perfect for me. I found perfection, *cara*. I'm not giving it up." His breath doesn't even hitch as he speeds up his thrusts. "You're mine, you understand?"

It's too much. I need him, need to come.

"Yes yes yes…" Each word is a pleading whisper and he kisses me, then drags his lips down to my ear, breathing there softly as he moves deep inside me for what feels like forever. I'm a wound harp string, ready to snap.

"You may come—" he says, and something inside me snaps. My body shudders hard through an orgasm. My knees grip his hips. He groans a half-second after me, and his hips beat a tattoo against mine as he comes hard inside of me.

My chest is heaving hard enough for the both of us, and I grip the ties binding me to the bed. Why do I feel so safe underneath him? Why does it feel so right?

"Good girl," he murmurs. "You did so well. You're perfect for me." He kisses my brow. My eyes fall closed. I'm tired, and the orgasm worked as a soporific, drugging me. He rises and unties me, returning to rearrange me in the bed.

The sheets and covers are surrounding me in his warmth and the soft scent of his cologne. This is where I belong, right here. I drift. His hands trace my curves, but I'm too tired to feel shy. His thumb strokes my belly. "You can't leave me, Leah. You might be pregnant with my child." His words are calm, but I hear an edge of hesitation in his voice, of antici-pation. That rouses me. My brows knot, my sex-wrung brain trying to think, but Royal's right. He didn't use protection.

You will be faithful to me, and bear my children.

"I've been careful with you, but no longer," he says. "I know you're clean."

How does he know that? I feel so fuzzy, I don't even speak the words.

"And I got tested," Royal says. "I'm clean too."

"I don't understand," I mumble.

"You will. I'll make sure of it." He kisses me again, and his murmur follows me into sleep. "My beautiful Leah."

* * *

LEAH

MY HAND FEELS HEAVY. That's the first sensation that enters my sleep-fogged mind. I crack my eyes open. I turn my hand over from where it's resting on the sheets, and light flares into my eyes.

There's a ring on my finger, sparkling in the soft ray of sunlight criss-crossing the bed. My lips part, my breath coming in rapid puffs. The starring gem is a huge princess cut diamond, blinding me when it catches the light. It's set in white gold and surrounded by a whole circle of smaller diamonds, as if one diamond weren't enough. The main rock is big enough to knock someone out if I slapped them, if I was the violent type.

I scramble out of bed. I'm alone again. Royal left me to

nap. The clock reads five p.m. Royal is probably working, or buying me more clothes, or announcing our engagement to the world. He probably thought the diamond on my finger gave him the last word.

It's a pretty effective argument. So are the faint red marks on my wrists and ankles and the soreness between my legs.

You belong to me.

I have an insane desire to run down to Royal's kitchen and bake up a storm. I haven't eaten today, right? I haven't felt hungry yet, but my stomach's finally waking up.

Chocolate, that's what I need. Chocolate will make everything better.

I go to the closet and exhale, trying to pick an outfit from the many beautiful clothes. The ring flashes at me every time I move my hand. There's a churning in my stomach, something between excitement and apprehension. Annoyance at how presumptuous he was, to put a ring on me, while I was asleep. Nervousness because I don't know how I'm going to talk my way out of this. A sick feeling, because if I can talk my way out of this, it's going to break my heart.

I rifle through the sweaters, and pick one out that's candy lilac, with rainbow threads dripping down the sleeves. I also grab black yoga pants because if I'm going to tell Royal off for putting a diamond the size of a ping-pong ball on my hand, I need to be ready to rumble.

I burst into Royal's office like a tornado, and he turns in his chair.

His face softens when he sees me, but before he can rise, I point an accusing finger at him.

"You," I say. His eyebrows slide upward and his lips quirk, like he's hiding a grin.

"Me?" He looks around the empty room, his expression playful. I like every side of Royal. Protective Royal.

Dangerous Royal. Tender Royal. Sexy as FUCK Royal. Royal in complete control. And this, Playful Royal.

On a lesser man, his smile would be a shit-eating grin. On him, it's just attractive and makes my belly melt.

"Did you think, for a minute, I might want to be awake for the proposal?" I ask, fluttering my hand in the air.

His eyes go soft and warm. "I couldn't risk you running again. There's a tracking device in there."

"Tracking device?" I squeak, when I find my voice.

"Oh yes," he murmurs. "You will not escape me again."

I put a hand to my forehead and the diamond clunks against my brow.

"Leah." He holds out an imperious hand. "Come here."

My legs are moving before I can stop them. I cross the room and he pulls me close.

"Good girl," he breathes, wrapping me in his arms and kissing me. "Happy Valentine's Day." He sinks into a large leather armchair and turns me so I'm sideways in his lap. We both stare down at my ring finger and the diamond winking at us. "I told you you would no longer be alone."

There's an explosion where my brain used to be. "Royal, please. I need answers."

"This is your engagement day, so I will entertain you and your theories."

"I don't have theories, I have questions," I say, my anxious fluttering simmering down somewhat. He's relaxed right now, this quiet time just for the two of us. He's back in his usual outfit of crisp shirt and black slacks. His sleeves are rolled up, showing off his taut forearms. I want to trace my fingers the length of his muscles, ruffle the dark hairs.

"Ask, whatever you want," he says, lifting my hand to his lips. He kisses my palm gently and I yank it away. I will not be distracted. Not right now.

"You say you want to marry me…" I stop because saying the word out loud is so unbelievable.

"I will marry you."

Okay. I swallow. "As your wife, what will I be expected to do?"

"Bake for me, naked."

I roll my eyes.

"I'm serious, baby. You do whatever you want to do as long as you spend the nights with me," he says, kissing my hand again. "Your nights are mine."

That shoots off distant, muted alarm bells in the back of my head.

What about his days? If he doesn't care about my days, where is he spending *his* days? With beautiful women? My heart already feels like it's going to shatter, and I must have stopped breathing because he takes me by the chin, gentle fingers on my skin.

"Leah?" he asks, concern on his face.

"I'm—" How will I know he's mine? My gaze travels past him to the fireplace mantle, to the collection of heavy, polished silver frames. Right in front is a picture of Royal with the statuesque, dark-eyed beauty. That's the kind of woman he should be with. She's poised and beautiful. There's more than one photo of him and her—some of them in a group, one of her and him alone. In each picture, they look good together. They look like they belong.

When I look back up at Royal, his forehead is furrowed.

"Who is that woman?" I'm bold enough to ask.

"My cousin. Lucrezia."

"Cousin?" Oh. Of course. She looks a lot like Royal and the rest of his cousins. Silly me, spiraling for no reason.

"We call her Lula," he says, affection plain in his voice. "You'll meet her… in about an hour," he says.

"What?" I shoot up off his lap, but he pulls me back.

"I asked her to come. She's my lawyer and I have some business. No, stay," he secures me in his lap, "I need you here."

"For business?" I ask, and squirm when his hand delves between my legs.

His lips find my ear. "Among other things." He's doing that thing again, with the palm of his hand. If I let him, he'll play me like a fiddle for the next thirty minutes, my brains will leak from my head when I come, and I won't get a chance to question him at all.

I push his hand away. "Royal, you've got to stop. I need you to talk to me. This whole Batman schtick only works in movies, the strong 'n silent schtick doesn't work for—"

He leans down and plants his mouth on mine, swallowing my words. My breath ends in a moan. The waking flower of warmth between my thighs has me rocking closer.

It's not fair. He knows exactly how to kiss me to muffle any protest I might have.

"But… Lula… business…"

"She's wonderful, and she's looking forward to meeting you."

"Oh my god, Royal, I can't do this."

"You can. You will. You're strong, Leah. Stronger than you know. Perfect for me." He silences me again with his tongue.

"Cookies," I gasp when I come up for air. "I need to bake something. Now."

"All right, *principessa*," he murmurs against my mouth. "You can bake something. You can do whatever you like, as long as you stay with me."

CHAPTER 7

 eah

THE FRONT DOOR opens to a chorus of muffled voices. I freeze, then shake my head and finish washing the big mixing bowl I used. The muffins are almost done. They're cranberry and chocolate chip. I love breakfast foods that are secretly dessert.

Royal spent the first half of the baking session lounging in the doorway, watching me with a half-lidded eyes. He looked so smug, I had to ask, "These baking things... did you buy them for me? Like the clothes?"

"Yes."

"It's too much."

He sauntered closer and cupped my face, ignoring the flour puffing around us. "Nothing is enough for my wife."

Then he kissed me and my brain short-circuited. I managed to order him out of the kitchen to give me a few blissful minutes to myself.

Now I'm about to meet Royal's cousin, and I'm covered in flour. *Oh well.* I might as well embrace who I am. I can't be anyone else.

The voices round the hall and a brunette with sleek, straight hair and wearing a black pantsuit walks in, followed by Royal. I feel short and shabby in my sugar-dusted outfit.

Lula is more beautiful in person, dark and striking like Royal. She could be his sister.

"So you're Leah," she says, looking me up and down. Her expression is inscrutable, and I don't know what she's thinking. "I'm his cousin," she explains, although I'm sure Royal's already told her that I know who she is. "Royal has a lot of cousins." The two of them exchange a look, and I can't tell if there's some secret meaning there, or an old joke.

"Okay," I say, trying not to sound as awkward as I feel.

"It's good to meet you." She sets down her slim leather briefcase. The Prada stamp is visible on the corner of it. That's a five thousand dollar briefcase. My brain blue screens.

Lula is offering me her hand. I grab it, my wet fingers sliding against her perfectly manicured ones.

"Oh sorry, I was just washing up." I get a dish towel and hand it to her. I use too much force and it flies out of my grip and nearly hits her in the face. "Oh my god, I'm sorry!"

"That's okay." Her dark eyes twinkle. "She cooks and cleans?" Lula raises a brow at her cousin.

"Only if she wishes." Royal crosses to my side and takes my left hand. His expression goes scarily blank.

"It's on the windowsill," I blurt. "I didn't want to lose it while washing dishes." The ring probably costs more than a year of Mr. Rossi's rent.

Royal collects the ring and takes my hand to slide it firmly onto my finger. "This stays on your finger," he murmurs. "Understand?"

"Once again, you didn't ask me," I tease, fluttering my fingers. The ring feels right on my hand. It's so pretty. I'm ignoring the little fact that it contains a tracking device—for now.

"Leah," Royal warns. His thumb strokes over my wrist.

"I understand. No more washing dishes. That'll be your job." I bump him with my hip.

"That can be arranged. I'm good at making things clean." *After I make things dirty,* his dark gaze adds.

Behind us, Lula clears her throat. I step back from the cocoon of warmth Royal and I created, my cheeks flushed from our flirting.

Lula holds up her phone. "Hey, cuz, Enzo's trying to reach you."

Royal pulls his own phone out of his pocket. "I'll be right back."

"I'll stay and get to know Leah," Lula says.

Royal runs a finger over my breastbone, swiping up sugar. He holds my gaze as he licks his finger. "Sweet."

I shiver.

"Be good," he warns, and stalks from the kitchen.

"Well, well." Lula fans herself. "That was unexpected." There's a real smile on her face. My heartrate slows. Somewhat. A little bit.

She leans on the marble island. "I've never known him to be so romantic."

"Really?" I wrinkle my nose, even though internally, I'm freaking out. "He's the most romantic guy I know."

"Maybe with you."

I don't know how to handle that, so I grab a drying pan and wipe it down with a dishrag.

"How did you two meet?" Lula asks.

"I served him coffee. Um, a few days ago."

The oven buzzer sounds and I busy myself taking out the

trays and setting out the muffins on racks to cool. Lula watches with narrowed eyes. Is she judging me? Or is she just thinking?

I set a muffin on a small plate. The chocolate and dried cranberry mixture turned out well. "Do you want one?"

"Absolutely." She wastes no time tearing off the paper liner and breaking the muffin open, cooing at the delicious steam. "This is amazing. I didn't know Royal had anything other than takeout menus in this kitchen."

"He said he bought the stuff for me." Of course he did. He's not the type to have muffin tins lying around.

"Oh my god, that's good," Lula moans. "No wonder Royal wants to marry you."

"You know about that?"

"It's kind of obvious." She nods to the giant diamond on my finger. "That, and the way he looks at you. I've never seen him like this with anyone."

"Really?" I lean on the island, picking at my own muffin, hungry for nothing but details about Royal. "I'd think women would be all over him."

"They are," Lula says with her mouth full.

She can't seem to eat her muffin fast enough, and that relaxes me even more. I can get along with anyone who likes my food.

"My cousin doesn't pay attention. He doesn't date. He barely notices women." She stabs the air with a manicured finger. "I take that back. There was someone he mentioned. Someone he met at a coffee shop."

"Oh?" I try to keep my voice casual, but the blood is roaring in my ears.

"Yeah. A girl who helped him last year's Valentine's Day. Her boyfriend had just broken up with her but she saw Royal was bleeding and bandaged his hands." Lula tilts her head. "Was that you?"

I lick my lips. Dumped before Valentine's Day? Sounds like me. But wouldn't I remember helping someone like Royal? "I don't know. I don't remember."

"Hmm." Lula pouts at her empty plate and picks at the remaining crumbs. "Must have been some other *panetteria*. Anyway," she dusts off her hands, seemingly unaware of the bomb she's dropped on my head, "I'm glad he found you."

"I don't know what's going on," I blurt. "I just met him a few days ago and now… he says he's going to marry me?"

"I'd believe him." Lula's poking around the kitchen. She opens a tin and fishes out one of the cookies I baked last night. "He's already booked the church."

I crumple a dish towel in my hands. "I'm waiting for him to tell me this is all a misunderstanding."

Lula takes a bite of the cookie. Her lashes flutter rapidly. "Wow, that's good," she mutters. She points the remaining cookie at me. "I wouldn't hold my breath if I were you. Once Royal gets an idea into his head, he doesn't tend to let it go. He's always been like that, ever since he was a child. Drove his father crazy," she adds in a mutter.

"Did you grow up with him?"

"No, we were together a lot when we were young, but then his dad shipped him off to the Old Country. He grew up with my aunt. She raised him. Uncle Vinnie—that's Royal's dad—swore he'd never let Royal run the family, but Auntie B pulls more strings from across the pond than Uncle Vinnie would like." Lula tilts her head, like she's dispensing a secret. "She doesn't get along with her brother. Between you and me, not many of us are fans of Uncle Vinnie, but he's the boss so we all toe the line. Except for Royal."

"Oh," I murmur, because what else can I say?

Lula crunches on the last of the cookie. "I don't know what he's planning but you're a part of it."

I gulp. I wanted more information, and I got it. But now

I'm sorry I did. I expected a sip of water and got a blast from a firehose.

"Doesn't Royal need a woman who's more..." I stop because I don't know what I'm going to say. More suited to the role of his wife? More beautiful or knowledgeable about his life?

"More what?" Lula's eyes soften, but Royal returns, strolling back into the kitchen and standing between us.

"It's time," he says and holds a hand. And even though I have no idea what's going on, what this beautiful man is about or why he's so set on making me his, I walk to him and put my hand in his.

Lula follows us to his office, a quiet smile on her face. Together, their height is intimidating. They're two tall book-ends and I'm the bedraggled kitten between them. *One of these things is not like the others. One of these things doesn't belong.*

Royal settles me in his huge desk chair. He takes my hand, checking for the ring. He runs a thumb over the jewel. "Did you and Lula have a good chat?"

"Yes?"

The two of them chuckle at my hesitation.

"So, Leah, in addition to being Royal's cousin, I'm also the family lawyer." Lula has her briefcase back in hand. She pulls a packet of papers out. "I drew up the papers you requested, we just need to sign them."

"I can go," I say, trying not to look too eager to get out of here, and appear like I'm jumping at reasons to bail.

"*Un momento*, Leah," Royal says. "We will need your witness and signature."

I huff under my breath—*foiled*—and look around the room while he sits and signs paper after paper. There's a thick stack of it, creamy-white and plush. I glance around the room, trying to act casual.

"Leah," Royal calls and pushes it towards me. "Now your signature."

"Do I want to know what I'm signing?" I mutter as I sign and initial the places Lula points out with her blood-red nails.

"My last will and testament," Royal says, off-hand.

"What?" My pen pauses, but I've already signed the last spot. "Am I witness?" I blink at him.

"No. You're my heir."

"What?" I shriek, and the pen drops from my ice-cold fingers. It thumps on the desk-top, and rolls before falling right off of the desk onto the floor.

Lula's already bundled the papers and stacked them neatly—oblivious, or politely ignoring my outburst. I gape at Royal.

"What—"

The study door opens and an older man bursts in. "I see I'm too late to stop this nonsense."

He's shorter, stockier, but his features are similar to Royal's. This is Vinnie, Royal's father. They have the same Roman nose. Vinnie's hair is streaked with gray, and he's got a spare tire he's been working on for a while. He's followed by two men, in long black wool coats, and dark sunglasses.

"Enough of this, Royal," Vinnie says, glancing at me for a moment before his gaze flicks away. Like I'm nothing, and nobody important. I shrink in the big leather chair, feeling even more like a kid playing 'office' in her father's study.

Lula is silent, snapping the papers into her briefcase. *Between you and me, not many of us are fans of Uncle Vinnie, but he's the boss so we all toe the line.*

Crap. This is the boss.

When Vinnie speaks again, and Lula looks at him for the first time, it's clear that not only doesn't she like him... she *loathes* him.

Royal's face has gone blank.

"You were meant for better things than this. The family has a reputation to uphold. You need to marry the daughter of a Don, maybe a Vesuvi or Serpente. One of the ruling families. Not someone like..." He waves a dismissive hand in my direction.

Lula's eyes narrow, her blood-red talons digging into the fine leather of her briefcase handle. I want to tell her not to bother getting mad on my behalf. I'm not worth it.

"Stop talking," Royal murmurs. His voice is low and deceptively soft. He's the type who doesn't get loud when he's furious. He gets quiet. It's the calm before the storm. I can feel it bubbling under the surface. Lula doesn't say anything either, but she's a little more obvious with her expression—a clear look of disdain on her face directed at one and only one human in the room. Together, she and Royal look formidable. Two sleek Doberman pinschers, focused on the kill.

Royal raises a hand.

Royal's father doesn't see the clues. He keeps talking, like he hasn't noticed his son and niece are furious with him. "There are families who would hand you their heirs on a silver platter. What the fuck are you doing with her? She's a nobody."

I flinch like I've been struck with a dagger.

One moment, Royal's leaning back against his desk, his hands gripping the edge, his dark head down. The next, he's exploded into silent motion. He crosses the few steps between them in a blur. His punch comes out of nowhere. His fist thunks into his father's face, and Vinnie flies back into a bookcase.

Books tumble around Vinnie. He grabs the shelves to right himself, groaning. The bodyguards freeze but make no move to defend the older Regis.

Of everyone, Lucrezia looks the least surprised. She examines her nails, casually, sighing the sigh of someone who's witnessed this type of scene before. I half expect her to get out a file to begin shaping one nail casually, maybe into a point. I tremble.

"Enough," Royal growls. He's not even breathing hard, his shoulders straight and spine stiff. "You're speaking of my bride. This was a test. You failed, Vinnie," he says to his father. The older man groans. "You're no longer my father. You rejected me, I reject you. It's that simple." Royal's eyes are hard, and Lula crosses her arms over her chest, staring down at her uncle. She looks completely unimpressed.

Something big is going on here, but I have no idea what it is. I'm grateful I'm not Daddy Regis. Even his bodyguards don't look like they want to come to his side in support.

He must be a *really* big asshole.

"You won't get away with this," Vinnie says, struggling to sit up. One of the bodyguards takes pity, and reaches down to help him up.

"I already have. Your sister sides with me. I have the support of the Old Country. And when I marry Leah tomorrow, I will have fulfilled the conditions of *La Famiglia*." Royal's eyes light up as he glances over to me. I cover my mouth with a hand. My left hand. The ring flashes its light around the room.

A hand comes to rest on my shoulder, and I look up. Lula's leaning over me, gripping my shoulder, her furious gaze glued to Vinnie Regis.

"They'll never accept her," Vinnie spits.

Royal shakes his head. "The crown has passed. The throne is mine."

His father makes a noise of rage in the back of his throat. "This isn't over." He shoots a final glare straight at me.

I flinch.

"Get out," Royal orders, and Vinnie does, followed by his two goons.

We listen to the front door open and close. There's a minor commotion, and Enzo jogs up to the office door, out of breath.

"Sorry boss," Enzo pants. "They took out Jimmy. Knocked him unconscious."

"Fuck." Lula whips her briefcase off Royal's desk. "I've got a med kit in my car."

"Go." Royal waves a hand to them both. "Secure the perimeter."

Lula and Enzo file out.

I bury my face in my hands.

"Leah." Royal's voice is soft. He sinks to his knees in front of me. "I'm sorry you had to see that."

"It's okay," I whisper. I can't deal with what just happened so I ask the first thing that's been bothering me. "You met me a year ago?"

"I didn't think you'd remember."

"I don't. Lula told me. I'm sorry, I was going through a break up and—"

"It's okay, *cara*. You've been through a lot. But you still took the time to help a man who was bleeding."

I take his hand, the one he used to hit his father. The red knuckles spark a memory in me. A wild-haired man in a dark, dusty coat. His face was bruised, his lip puffy and broken. I had thought he was homeless. He did have beautiful dark eyes. Was that Royal?

"I'd just survived an attack. I wasn't fit to be seen. But you saw me." He clasps my hand, turning it over so the diamond winks between us. "And I saw you. I knew the right woman was out there, waiting for me. And then there you were." His whisper is pure sin, silky and intimate. "No one else seemed to notice you. But I did." Like everything he says, this causes seismic shifts inside me. "I would've come to you sooner, but it wasn't safe. Not until I had more of a foothold."

He's talking about gangs and turf wars again, things over my head.

I swallow. "Your father—"

"He's losing power." Royal sounds dismissive.

"He doesn't approve of me."

"He doesn't matter."

"But what he said…" I close my eyes and let the tears fall.

"No, Leah. Do not cry over what he said." Royal braces me in his strong arms, bundling me into his lap. His chair dips as he leans back, holding my head to his chest. My tears spot his white shirt.

"Poor *principessa*. I'll make him pay for what he did to you."

"I'm okay," I sniffle. Royal presents a handkerchief and I give a half laugh. Trust Royal to be a mix of modern and old world courtesies.

I fix my gaze on his beautiful face while he dries my tears. His warmth and scent anchor me.

"I didn't speak until I was four years old." He tips my face this way and that, examining it for tears. "My father thought I was a failure. He sent me away."

"He was wrong," I say.

"Yes." Royal grips my chin. "He's wrong about most things."

A sigh shudders out of me, and I nod.

"Forget him," Royal orders. "He's nothing. You're everything."

"You just need to marry someone," I say before I can stop myself. He scowls and glances away then shakes his head.

"I want to marry you. At first, I looked for a bride who would know her place beside me. Someone from one of the three other families, someone convenient. But the more I watched you, the more I knew how perfect you would be. I need someone like you at my side." He rubs his thumb up and down my finger gently, cherishing even this small part of me. "When I am with you, I feel it. Fate," he finishes.

I blink at him through wet lashes. "What if I need more than fate?" I ask, but I'm wavering. He's never let me down. Not in the short time I've known him. He's been so fiercely protective of me, of anyone even tangentially related to me.

He treats me like I'm someone special. Even if I have my reservations, I'm not strong enough to give that up.

"Fate brings us together," he says, "you and me? We get to write the rest of it together. Fate leaves the fun parts for us to discover." My heart thumps in my chest and he leans in to kiss me. I let him, and he slowly kisses across my face, brushing away any tears that are left.

"I don't know," I whisper.

"Trust me," he says. I let my eyes fall closed. He wants me to believe that I'm the best choice for him. I can trust him, but can I trust in the truth of us?

I can try. For Royal, I will try.

* * *

LEAH

THE WEDDING DRESS FITS PERFECTLY.

I can't believe I'm doing this. But Royal asked me to trust him, and now I'm wearing all of the lace that exists in our state, what with the veil, shoes, bralette and garter belt holding up sheer stockings. And then the crowning glory of it all, the dress itself, a bespoke explosion of tulle and satin. I turn and peer at myself in the mirror, a glittering backdrop of expensive shoes and handbags behind me.

I look like a giant cupcake with too much vanilla frosting. I try to pull the veil one way, and then the other. Am I really doing this?

Lula is also here, trying on bridesmaid dresses. Royal has left the house to attend to business.

"Whoa," she says when I emerge from the walk-in closet. The suite two doors down from Royal's master bedroom looks like a bridal shop, and it's been turned into one for our benefit to prep for the wedding tomorrow. "That's… a lot of tulle."

"I know." I wrinkle my nose.

"It's not so bad. You do look beautiful." Speaking of beautiful, Lula is gorgeous, in a trumpet gown that falls to the floor in a deep wine red that suits her coloring. She approaches me and gingerly touches the tulle that's frothing around my knees, adjusting it here and there. "Hmmm," she says gently, before pinching at my veil. "There, now what do you think?" she asks, and we turn to the mirror.

My eyes widen. There's something about the way she's adjusted the fall of the veil, and arranged my train behind me—

I look like a princess. My cheeks flush. I look like a bride.

The woman in the mirror doesn't look like the girl with pastry baking dreams. She looks like a goddess.

She looks nothing like me.

"You're good at this," I say to Lula. "If you ever get sick of being a lawyer, you could be a stylist."

Lula laughs. She laughs easily, which is another point in her favor.

"It's easy when the bride's so beautiful," she says, and her words warm my heart. She doesn't have to be nice to me. She doesn't owe me anything, not even kindness. But here we are, the day before I get married, and she's fussing over me like I'm her sister, not a woman she just met who's now her cousin's fiancée.

Uncertainty wells up inside me again. No matter how tight Royal holds me at night, I still feel out of place. A raisin in a chocolate chip cookie. Like one day, Royal will wake up and see the shy, shabby girl he's chosen, and send me back to the bakery where I belong.

I wish I could be more like Lula. Calm, collected Lula.

"Enzo said that Royal has to get married so he can take over the family," I blurt.

Lula tilts her head to the side, studying me. "Yes. That is true. He also used you to force a confrontation with his father."

"What?" I whisper.

Lula circles me, tweaking my voluminous train. "One thing you need to know about Royal. He never does anything that doesn't net him multiple results. Two, three, ten times the returns. That's why the family is so eager to give him what he wants. They will do anything to keep him happy, and you make him happy."

I press a hand to my forehead. The diamond is heavy on my finger.

"I don't know what to do," I whisper.

"Leah, as long as I've known my cousin, I've never known him to be this obsessed with anyone. It'll work out. You'll see." She finishes tweaking my veil and steps back. "I've got to go. Want me to unzip you?"

"Uh, no, I'll wear it a bit longer." Maybe if I wear it, I'll get used to it.

"You sure?" Lula says. "It's bad luck for the groom to see you."

"I don't think anything will derail Royal from making this wedding happen." I smooth a hand down the beautiful bodice.

Lula's smile is bright enough for the both of us as she goes to unzip her bridesmaid dress. "You're right. He doesn't believe in luck. He believes in fate."

The house is extra quiet when Lula leaves. Standing and staring at myself in a wedding dress is doing nothing for my confidence. The woman glowing under the soft lights of the guest bedroom before a sea of fine dresses looks nothing like me. I should have let Lula unzip me. Then I could get back to the kitchen and procrasti-bake.

Downstairs, a door slams.

I hitch up the tulle and start walking down the stairs, careful not to step on my train. "Royal?"

Downstairs is dark. I descend into shadows, and when I get to the bottom of the steps, I round the railing in the direction of the front door.

Five feet from me is the slumped form of one of Royal's bodyguards, his gun on the ground beside his limp hand. I catch the scent of stale cigarettes.

I whirl. At the back of the walk-in closet in Royal's bedroom is a safe room. He showed it to me just the other morning in a brief tour, telling me to go there if there was ever a problem. Another freaky mafia wife lesson I need to learn.

Two steps up the stairs, I trip on the tulle.

"I don't think so," someone says, and seizes me around the waist. I shriek and drive my elbow backward into a firm belly. The man grunts and then claps a hand over my mouth, a cloth fisted in his fingers. I inhale the fumes, antiseptic and sweet. My head fogs over, my vision clouding, and that's all—

CHAPTER 8

My head throbs like someone's driven a nail through my temple. My cheek is pressed to a scratchy surface. Voices murmur over my head. Male voices.

My heart slams in my ribcage, and I jolt awake. I'm still in the wedding dress. The veil has flopped over my face. I brush it aside.

I'm lying on faded green and yellow cushions, on what's got to be the ugliest plaid couch in existence. The room is musty, with dust motes dancing in the dim sunbeams. The walls are fake wood paneling.

"What?" I mumble with a painfully dry mouth.

"She's awake," someone mutters, and stale cigarette smoke wafts over me.

I push myself up and lean back on the couch. A dark figure looms over me.

Vinnie Regis. Royal's dad.

"Where am I?" I mutter.

"Welcome to my humble abode." Vinnie flicks his cigarette, and ash flies onto the matted brown carpet. "Not as nice as Royal's place, is it? Course, his place used to be mine.

What sort of son pushes his father out?" Spittle flies out his mouth. He raises a hand to push back his hair. He's holding a gun.

I press myself into the couch.

"Fucker always was a silent freak of a kid, always plotting." Vinnie notices me cowering in a cream puff of a dress. "I don't know what he sees in you." His lip curls. "*La Famiglia* isn't gonna allow their golden prince to marry some nobody. If he goes through with this—" he waves his gun at my poofy white dress, "they'll reject him. I'm doing him a favor, taking you."

I lick my lips. *Stay calm. Stay calm. Channel Lula.* "What are you going to do with me?"

"Keep you a while, teach him a lesson. Make him trade you for the territory he took from Stefanos. Stefanos was cutting me in." Vinnie keeps ranting. His men hover around him, nodding and smirking at me.

I close my eyes. *Do not cry.* I press my thumb against the band of my engagement ring. Royal will come for me.

I just have to hold on until then.

"Can I use the bathroom?" I rasp once Vinnie's stomped out of the room. One of the goons left to watch me shrugs and points out a door in the wood paneled walls.

In the bathroom, I scoop water into my hands and drink my fill. Twitching my skirts away from the filthy tile, I lean over the sink and stare at my reflection. "Think, Leah." A goddess with big brown eyes blinks back at me. She looks calm, in control. Ready to get married.

Royal is going to come for me, and I need to be ready. If I see an opportunity to escape, I need to take it. Maybe I can manufacture a distraction.

I open the medicine cabinet and stare at the contents. I can figure this out.

I keep my head down when I exit the bathroom. Vinnie is

back, lighting a new cigarette. I clasp my hands in front of me.

"Can I use your kitchen?"

"For what?" Vinnie blows smoke in my direction.

I shrug. "I'm a baker. I like baking. I want to make cupcakes. I always do that on Valentine's Day, but didn't get to yesterday."

Vinnie's bushy brows rise. I try to look meek and scared. Unassuming. Out of my depth. I don't have to try hard.

"Whatever. Make yourself at home. But don't get any ideas." He motions to one of his men. "Take all the knives outta there."

Vinnie's goon precedes me to the yellow kitchen and yanks open a silverware drawer, pulling out all the knives. My skirts swish over faded linoleum. "Thank you," I murmur, keeping my eyes downcast. I find an apron that's clean besides a few old stains, and put it on over my dress.

In what feels like no time at all, I'm turning off the oven buzzer and pulling out my creations. A few goons have gathered in the living room, drawn by the vanilla scent. I swan over to the dusty dining room table and set down a full plate of pink cupcakes.

"How'd you get them pink?" Vinnie asks, suspicion written on his face.

Blood in the frosting. "I found a little bottle of food coloring. You can have as many as you like," I say. "I already had mine." I point to a demolished pile of crumbs and baking paper. I did pretend to eat a cupcake, so as not to arouse suspicion.

The men fall on them. Even Vinnie eats one. Pink frosting smears his face. My cupcakes are too good to be ignored.

While the men are eating their fill, I putter around the kitchen for a few minutes, pretending to clean up. Then I take off my apron and visit the downstairs restroom again before sitting on the edge of the ugly couch in the front room, my hands folded in my lap like a good little girl. The wedding dress poofs around me.

Under the mix of cigarette fumes and the pleasant smell of cake, there's a slight stench of rotten eggs starting to build up. It's very faint. No one should notice it, unless they're looking for it.

I watch the cheap clock askew on the wall. The seconds tick by.

It doesn't even take a half hour, like it said on the box. Fifteen minutes in, the first mafioso groans and staggers to the bathroom.

This is the dangerous part. If Vinnie catches on and orders someone to put a bullet in my head for what I've done, it's all over.

But he doesn't. From the moans and groans all over the house, he and his men are making good use of the bathroom. In the closest bathroom there's also some hacking and coughing. The toilet bowl cleanser I dumped in with the bleach in a stopped up tub must have produced some toxic gas.

I need to get out of here, fast.

I stand and step lightly over the creaking floorboards. The front door is wide open like someone rushed inside and forgot to shut it. They were probably trying to make it to a toilet before shitting their bowels out.

I don't have a phone or a car, but I glide out the door and start up the gravel drive towards the road. I make a great target in my white dress. Hopefully all the mafiosos are occupied trying not to die on the toilet. Or the other distractions I've set up will keep them occupied.

Inside the house, people are swearing. Someone in the bathroom upstairs is praying to God, loudly.

I'm a few quick steps down the walk when the fire alarm

in the kitchen starts to beep. The mix of oil and crumbs I poured in the toaster oven finally did its job. Smoke's pouring out of the kitchen, which means the bag of flour and sheaf of old newspapers I shoved in the oven are probably about to catch fire.

I pick up my skirts and start to run.

There are shouts behind me. A few shots ring out, and I duck, still rushing away from the house as fast as I can in this huge dress. I guess the laxatives wore off.

Royal's dad is on the front lawn, gun in hand. He tries to take aim even as his face contorts and he folds over his cramping stomach, bending double. He's pretty determined to shoot me, even as he's shitting himself.

I hoist my skirts higher and force myself to pick up speed. I run like the house behind me is on fire.

I'm at the top of the road when a giant booming blast makes me stagger. I get to my feet. Royal's dad is prone on the lawn, still moaning. Still alive.

Flames roar in the space that used to be the house's kitchen. The fire quickly spreads. Thugs pour from the windows and doors onto the lawn, hacking in the thick smoke. Most are bent in half like their colons are still rioting.

A black SUV screeches up to me. Royal jumps out the back, a gun in his hand. "Leah!" His black hair and eyes are wild, but he tucks the gun away as he strides to me.

Then I'm in his arms.

"It's okay," I murmur. "I'm all right. He didn't hurt me."

Royal crushes me to him, burying me in his wool coat. He jerks his head towards the house, and Enzo and the rest of his men head towards it.

"No!" I gasp. "Wait!"

"Shhh, *principessa mia,*" Royal says, trying to bundle me into the car.

"You can't go in there," I shout to Enzo and the rest. "Not yet. I messed with the gas lines."

Enzo and the men stop short.

In the distance, there's a whine of fire engine sirens.

"Come here." Royal scoops me up and sets me in the car. I fight through my crinkling skirt to grab his lapels. "Royal, I'm serious. They can't go near the house."

"They won't, baby. Give me a second." He tears himself away.

I collapse back into the car seat in a pile of white fabric. I did it. I survived.

Outside the car, Royal stands in a knot of his cousins, giving orders. His deep voice rises and falls. The sound is soothing. I could fall asleep, if I weren't so charged with adrenaline.

"*Principessa.*" Royal pushes into the car and pulls me into his arms, easily overcoming the wall of the wedding dress.

I pull my skirts out of the way so they won't catch in the door. "You know, for two hundred yards of tulle, this dress survived pretty well."

Royal cups my face, forcing me to focus. "Leah."

"It's okay." I press myself to him. "I'm okay."

He steals a kiss, murmuring against my lips, "I'll never forgive myself."

"It wasn't your fault. And everything turned out okay."

Enzo appears by the open car door. "Boss, you're not going to believe this. I had one of our men drive by and get intel. Looks like the firemen found illegal substances in the house. The cops arrived to take everybody in."

I bite my lip. Is it bad I got Royal's dad arrested?

"The guys all had their pants down," Enzo continues. "They ate some bad shit or something. It stunk so bad—"

"What the fuck?" Royal breathes.

Time to come clean. I duck my head and raise my hand, like a kindergartener in class. The men's eyes cut to me.

"I may have found an expired box of off-brand Ex-Lax and made cupcakes with them," I say.

"Fuck me," Enzo says with awe.

"I also, um, put a bag of flour in the oven, and oil in the toaster. And turned them on. Oh, and dumped bleach and ammonia into the bathroom. In addition to, um…" My voice dies to a whisper as Enzo's eyebrows creep upward. Royal's face is scarily blank. "Tampering with the gas line."

Enzo looks too overcome to swear. He opens his mouth, closes it, and crosses himself.

"Let me get this straight," Royal says. "You took down a house full of thugs using nothing but a smoking oven and cupcake mix."

"Excuse me, I bake everything from scratch." I'd never made laxative cupcakes before, but when my ex dumped me, I might have looked up a recipe a time or two.

Royal's brows are two angry slashes in his face. Is he mad at me?

"Tell me the truth, Leah," Royal rumbles. "Did you take out my father and a bunch of his men with homemade cupcakes?"

"No one expects stealth poop muffins," I whisper.

"Fuck me," Enzo says in a tone of awe.

The blaring sirens are coming closer.

"Uh, boss?" Another mafioso hovers behind Enzo. "We should get out of here before the cops widen the net."

"All right." Royal waves a hand. "Move out." He crushes me to his side. His lips burn a kiss to my browline. "I am taking you home."

CHAPTER 9

The girl in the mirror is glowing. She looks happy, even when she bites her lip. I'm back in a wedding dress—a different one from yesterday. The last one survived kidnapping and an escape from a gas explosion, but not Royal's passion. In his haste to undress me, not even the veil remained unripped.

"Yoohoo, Leah?" Lula sticks her head into the dressing room. "You ready to get married? I'm supposed to take you to the wedding. Royal has a last minute meeting with the family."

"Oh." A meeting with the family? I'm not sure if that's a good or bad thing.

"How are you doing?" Lula saunters in, looking fabulous in her bridesmaid dress.

"I'm good." I finger the lace of the new wedding dress. An Alonuko original. I have no idea how Royal got it custom made overnight.

"You sure? No lingering effects from yesterday?"

I flush. I am a little sore, but not from being held hostage. Royal was pretty eager to show me how glad he was that I was back safe and sound. And I was just as eager to reciprocate.

But I woke up alone. Royal left a note and a chocolate muffin, but I'd have preferred him.

"I'll take that as a no," Lula says with a grin. "You might be interested to know, I just came from the hospital. Royal's father and the rest of them need counsel." I stiffen, but Lula doesn't notice. She tosses her dark hair over shoulder. "I'm arranging plea bargains for all of them. The firemen and cops didn't like all the drugs they found. They're going to jail for a long time."

I bite my lip. This is good news, but will Royal be happy that I got his dad in trouble?

"We don't even have to bring kidnapping charges unless you really want to," Lula adds gently. "I figured you might want to stay out of it."

"I do," I say quickly.

"Then that's settled. I have to say it's my first time dealing with a situation like this. Typically, when I do hospital visits, my client has been shot, not taken out by a cupcake. But one of the guys is in critical condition. The rest are severely dehydrated."

"They ate a lot of cupcakes."

"Yeah they told me that." She snickers. "I had to fight to keep a straight face. I can't believe your plan worked."

I shrug. "No one suspected a thing. Pink cupcakes are the most innocuous thing on earth."

Lula shakes her head. "I told Royal he'd better watch himself with you."

"I only make laxative cupcakes in extreme situations."

"Good to know. But it might be a while before I eat anything else you bake."

"That's fair."

We share a grin.

"Seriously, Leah, you did good. A whole embarrassing branch of our family was taken out in one go. The three other crime families in Metropolis are watching. We needed a show of strength if we're going to take a seat at the table."

Lula moves to the mirror and straightens her dress, unaware that she's making my head spin.

"Royal's father was the weakest link, but now Royal has proven that he can clean house. And he did it without having to kill his father. What did I tell you?" Lula holds up her manicured fingers. "Royal needed a bride. He needed a reason to get rid of his father. And he wanted you. I told you." She taps her temple. "Royal has a brain like an engineer. He's always tinkering. Always fixing things in his head. His mind works like a clock."

"Right." I blow out a shaky breath.

"All right, let's head out." Lula grabs her Chanel purse and fishes for her keys. "I'm supposed to drive you to the church. Unless you want to blow off my cousin and head to Atlantic City?" Her tone is joking, but there's a serious assessment in her dark eyes.

"No." I smooth my hands down the bodice.

Lula's dark eyes search my face. "I'm serious, Leah. You don't have to marry him, if you don't want to. "

"I do want to." I might not be totally okay with everything in his world, but I want Royal. "But on the way to the church… is it okay if we make one stop?"

* * *

THE BAKERY IS a bright spot in the dark strip mall. Someone's replaced the old door and added a fresh coat of paint. The overhead sign is new and bigger, with pink lettering like I always wanted.

"You'll be okay?" Lula calls from her black Beemer. I nod

and pick up my skirts, trudging to the new front door. Once inside, I drop my train, unsure of what to do. The place smells like spices—red beans and rice, goat curry. Mrs. Rossi is cooking again.

"Leah!" Mr. Rossi bursts from the back, Mrs. Rossi right behind him. They sandwich me, taking turns giving me hugs. "Look at you!"

"Bellissima!"

"Ms. Rossi," I choke out. "You look great."

"The infusions are helping." She pats my cheek. Her hand is soft, her dark skin glowing. "Your man is a prince."

My throat closes. "Yes, he is."

"And now you are to be married. You make a beautiful bride."

"Thank you." I finger my veil. "Will you walk me down the aisle? Both of you?"

"Oh." Mrs. Rossi is so overcome, she puts a hand to her mouth.

Mr. Rossi puts a gentle arm around her. "We wouldn't miss it, *Mia figlia.*" *My daughter.* "We are headed to the church soon. We just put the finishing touches on the cake."

"You made my cake?"

He beckons, and I follow the Rossis to the back. The cake is a tower of white, tall enough to touch the heavens.

In the front room, the bell over the door jingles madly.

"That door should be closed." Mr. Rossi frowns.

I know who's just walked in before his velvety deep voice washes over me. "Mr. Rossi. Mrs. Rossi."

Firm hands grasp my hips.

Royal's found me. Of course he has.

"Call me Cedella." Mrs. Rossi beams.

"Come, my bride." Mr. Rossi puts his arm around his wife and starts steering her away. "We need to get to the church."

"We're right behind you," Royal mutters into my veil. He

holds me still until the shop door jingles closed. The Rossis are gone. It's just me and Royal now.

"You came," I say before I turn. He doesn't let me out of his grasp, but lets me face him. Good thing he hangs on because as soon as my eyes hit his, my knees wobble.

"You ran," he counters. His eyes are dark coffee, his beautiful face stern, but his expression softens when he sees my face. He picks me up, poofy satin dress and all, and carries me out to the baking cases. He sets me on the counter next to the espresso machine that started this all. My skirts overflow, but he crushes them down, planting his arms on either side of me and fixing me with a dark stare. "Leah."

"Royal," I say warily.

He tilts his head. "You wanted a coffee before we tie the knot?"

"I needed a moment," I whisper. My vision blurs and I blink a few times. "You fixed the shop. You fixed everything."

He runs a finger over my quivering lip. "Yes. I'd do anything for you."

"Your dad said the family won't like you taking me as a bride."

He shakes his head. "I just met with them. They can't wait to meet you. They approve of you."

"I am pretty badass." My voice wobbles, but the pride on Royal's face steadies me.

Maybe I can do this. Royal hinted at a honeymoon in the Old Country. I do want to meet Royal's aunt. I hope she'll approve of me. Maybe a tin of cookies is all I'll need to buy her love. I'll let Royal make the espresso.

My reflection in the espresso maker shows a bride. She looks calm, but inside, she's quivering.

Maybe that's okay.

"Talk to me, Leah." Royal smooths back my veil.

"You hired the Rossis to make the cake."

His glossy hair falls in his face as he shakes his head. "They wouldn't take payment. Wedding gift."

I stroke his hair out of his face.

"Mr. Rossi wanted to bake in his kitchen one last time."

My blood ices over. "What?" I whisper. Did they have to sell? Is that how they paid for the treatment? But I thought Cedella said Royal paid for it.

"They sold the business. With Cedella's health back, they want to travel more. Retire to Jamaica."

"They found a buyer."

"You could say I made them an offer they couldn't refuse."

"You?"

"This place. It's yours now. Consider it a Valentine's Day gift."

I tilt my eyes up so I don't cry. Once the tears slide back down, I say, "You're so sweet. I didn't get you anything."

"You're giving me everything. The only gift I want is this." He palms my pussy over the dress. "You're gonna come willingly to the church, or do I have to tie you up and carry you?"

I giggle. "I'll come."

"Good. Because if I had to throw you over my shoulder, first you'd be going over my knee."

A tingle runs through me. But I bite my lip.

"What are you thinking, *principessa?*"

"Are you mad about what I did to your father?"

"My father threw me away like trash because I wasn't the son he wanted."

"I hate him," I say with a vehemence that surprises me.

Royal doesn't seem surprised. He looks pleased. "There's some darkness in you, little one. Maybe that's why we fit so well. The bitter and the sweet." He lifts my hand and kisses it. The ring sparkles between us.

"You know," I say. "You never asked me to marry you."

"Do you want me to ask?" He leans forward, crushing my

skirts. His lips find my ear. "Do you want me to convince you, *cara?* Because I can be very persuasive."

"No, no," I say, but he's tossing up the hem of my dress. I rock back on the counter, propping myself on my elbows as he reaches under my satin skirts.

"Royal! We need to get to the church."

"*Un momento.*" He squeezes my stocking-clad knee, finding the garter belt strap and snapping it. "First, I want to make you scream."

I collapse back on the counter, knocking over a stack of paper cups. A cloud of white puffs over me—powdered sugar. When I lick my lips, they're sweet.

Royal presses two fingers into my pussy, the heel of his hand grinding against my clit. "Come for me, *cara*. And while you do, say my name. Tell me who owns you."

When I come, it's Royal's name on my lips.

* * *

AND THAT'S the story of why my train left a trail of confectioner's sugar as I walked between Mr. and Mrs. Rossi down the church aisle to become Mrs. Royal Regis.

EPILOGUE

oyal

A SHARP PAIN knifes up my side. My breath wheezes out. Under my jacket, my shirt is growing wet. My boots clunk over the broken black top. I want to stop and sink to the ground.

Got to keep moving.

The thug came out of nowhere, popping into my path and pulling me into a forced embrace. I wrenched myself away, but not before his knife sank into me, a red hot slash burning like wildfire through my core.

I'm bloody and bruised, but I'm in better shape than him. I left him in a dark pile by a dumpster.

The assassination was like everything my father's ever done. Sloppy.

E tu, padre?

The pink door of the bakery glimmers ahead of me, a mirage in the desert. My left eye is a bit blurry. Probably turning black. I force my feet to trudge on, staggering up the glass-strewn pavement. A pile of newspapers have spilled out of their glass case and turned into a sodden mass of pulp.

This was once a nice area, but crime and gangs have ruined its charm. Sent the townspeople packing. These shop owners pay for protection, but my father gives them nothing.

That's something I'll change.

My father thought he'd end things with a quiet knifing. What sort of man sends assassins to take out his own son?

He thinks he can best me. I'll take his mansion, his territory, and then I'll take his throne. Nothing can stop me. *La Familigia* will back the victor. The wheels and cogs in my head are turning. There's just one missing piece.

The bell over the bakery door rings out, announcing a customer leaving. I stop, leaning against the wall like an addict contemplating his next fix.

A young couple blows out of the bakery. Both are blond and laughing, arm in arm. They look like brother and sister, wearing matching Empire University sweatshirts. I wait for them to jump into their bright red Camaro and drive off before limping to the Panetteria door.

More of my father's assassins might be looking for me and I need a place to hide. They won't expect me to have walked this far on foot. I blink at my boots. Have I left a trail of blood? A knife in the gut will do that.

I push open the bakery door. The bell cha-chings and the sweet scent hits me. For a moment I'm back in *mia zia*'s kitchen, watching her roll out the dough with her floury arms jiggling.

A young woman stands behind the counter. Her eyes are red rimmed but she gives me a brave smile. "Hello, welcome to *Panetteria Principessa*." She pronounces the Italian perfectly. "What can I help you with?"

I straighten as best I can, limping to inspect the bakery cases. My reflection in the glass shows an unkempt man with sallow cheeks and dark crevices under his eyes. I look twenty years older than I am. I look like a homeless man.

I am a homeless man. For now.

Until I take my father's mansion. That will be my first move.

"*Un caffè, per favore.*" My voice is a guttural rasp.

She bustles to get it. I lean a little too heavily on the counter and when she returns, she nearly drops the cup.

"Oh my god," she says. "You're bleeding."

"It's nothing." I wave a hand and wince. "Do not trouble yourself."

"No, no, wait here." She whirls and heads to the door leading to the back of the shop. Through the haze of pain, I focus on her curvy backside.

The burn in my side fades to nothing. By the time she returns with a first aid kit, I'm standing taller.

"May I?" She gestures to my hand.

At my nod, she lifts it and begins to clean the slash on my palm with gentle hands. Funny, I didn't even feel that wound. The one under my jacket is much greater. What would this little baker do if I shrugged off my layers and showed her my red-stained shirt?

Up close, I can study her snub nose, her dark lashes, her bright doe eyes. She's been crying, but there's more color in her cheeks now than when I first came in.

"Did someone upset you?" I ask as she bandages the cut.

"Oh, it's nothing." She blinks and sniffles. "My boyfriend just broke up with me," she admits. "That was him and his new girlfriend who left just now. They acted like..." Her voice drops to a whisper. "They acted like I was nobody to them. We spent four years together in high school." Her voice wobbles. "Anyway."

She's upset, and still she gives what she can to me. A perfect stranger.

She reaches for a bakery box and sets one perfect, pink-frosted cupcake into it. "Happy Valentine's Day." She hands me the white box. There's the barest quiver in her lower lip. "I hope yours is better than mine."

"Thank you." It's all I can do not to leap over the counter to thank her properly, knife wound be damned.

I stroll to the door, bakery box in hand. I pause with my hand on the door and twist to ask her, "Do you believe in fate?"

Her brow furrows, but she doesn't say no.

A plan is brewing inside me. The puzzle I've been trying to solve, shifting and locking together.

She is the missing piece.

It's too soon to say this. "Something tells me next year's Valentine's Day will be better than this one."

"I hope so," she says.

I dip my head, and wrench the door open, striding into the day. Soon, I will return.

I'm coming for you, principessa.

WANT MORE LEAH & Royal? Read **A Bun In The Oven,** an exclusive extra scene starring Leah & Royal from *Revenge is Sweet*

By Lee Savino

"CARA," he groans. "You're perfect for me." Plunging his cock deep inside, the angle is just right, each pass rubbing my G spot. The deep sensation makes my legs quiver. "I'm going to tie you up and leave you at my mercy, and when the time is right,"—he slows his

thrusts, rolling his hips so I feel his every inch—"I'm going to breed you."

***

Go here to read it: https://geni.us/Abunintheoven
Then grab Mafia Brides book 2: https://geni.us/VengeanceisMine

JOIN THE VINO VILLAINI!

If you're a Booktok or Instagram influencer, I'd love you to apply to join my Influencer team.

Team members are eligible for ARCs, special edition books and other book mail, peeks behind the scenes, live launch parties and more!

Come join the fun! Become a Vino Villain today!

<3 Lee

Apply here: https://www.leesavino.com/influencers

Beauty's Beast
Beauty & the Thorns
Beauty & the Rose

* * *

Contemporary Romance

Royally Wrong
Royally Bad
Royally Fake Fiancé

Bad Boy Heroes
Her Marine Daddy
Her Dueling Daddies
Beauty & The Lumberjacks
Snowed in with the Lumberjack
Rescuing Regina

* * *

Paranormal romance

Berserker Saga
Sold to the Berserkers
Mated to the Berserkers
Bred by the Berserkers (FREE novella only available at
www.leesavino.com)
Taken by the Berserkers
Given to the Berserkers
Claimed by the Berserkers
Rescued by the Berserker
Captured by the Berserkers

Kidnapped by the Berserkers
Bonded to the Berserkers
Berserker Babies
Night of the Berserkers
Owned by the Berserkers
Tamed by the Berserkers
Mastered by the Berserkers
Surrendered to the Berserkers

Berserker Warriors
Aegir
Siebold with Ines Johnson

Bad Boy Alphas with Renee Rose
Alpha's Temptation
Alpha's Danger
Alpha's Prize
Alpha's Challenge
Alpha's Obsession
Alpha's Desire
Alpha's War
Alpha's Mission
Alpha's Bane
Alpha's Secret
Alpha's Prey
Alpha's Blood
Alpha's Sun

Shifter Ops with Renee Rose
Alpha's Moon
Alpha's Vow
Alpha's Revenge
Alpha's Fire

Alpha's Rescue
Alpha's Command

A Very Merry Alpha's Solstice

Bad Boy Bears with Renee Rose
Alpha's Claim

Midnight Doms with Renee Rose
Alpha's Blood
His Captive Mortal
The Virgin and the Vampire
(All Souls' Night anthology exclusive)

Werewolves of Wallstreet with Renee Rose
Big Bad Boss: Midnight
Big Bad Boss: Moon Mad
Big Bad Boss: Marked
Big Bad Boss: Mated
Big Bad Bully

* * *

Sci fi romance

Planet of Kings with Tabitha Black
Brutal Mate
Brutal Claim
Brutal Capture
Brutal Beast
Brutal Demon

Tsenturion Warriors with Golden Angel

Alien Captive
Alien Tribute
Alien Abduction

Dragons in Exile with Lili Zander
Draekon Mate
Draekon Fire
Draekon Heart
Draekon Abduction
Draekon Destiny
Daughter of Draekons
Draekon Fever
Draekon Rogue
Draekon Holiday

Draekon Rebel Force with Lili Zander
Draekon Warrior
Draekon Conqueror
Draekon Pirate
Draekon Warlord
Draekon Guardian

* * *

Cowboy Romance

Rocky Mountain Mail Order Brides
Rocky Mountain Dawn
Rocky Mountain Bride
Rocky Mountain Rose
Rocky Mountain Romp
Rocky Mountain Rogue
Rocky Mountain Daddy

Rocky Mountain Ride
Possessing Pearl

Wild Whip Ranch with Tristan River
Cowboy's Babygirl
Taming His Wild Girl

ABOUT THE AUTHOR

USA today bestselling author Lee Savino has written over 69 steamy romance novels. Bad boys, mafia men, wolf shifters, and dragon shifters in space—her dominant, alpha-hole heroes will stop at nothing to possess their one true love. Happily-ever-after and book hangover guaranteed!

Download a free book at leesavino.com.

Connect with Lee Savino in her fabulous Goddess Group: https://www.facebook.com/groups/LeeSavino

Goodreads: http://bit.ly/2tqaH28
Bookbub: http://bit.ly/2h8N6le
TikTok: https://www.tiktok.com/@authorleesavino
Instagram: https://www.instagram.com/authorleesavino